Little

Devil

By Joanne Alain Cook

JACbooks

Cover design by: Joanne Cook

For the night owls in my life, G, J, and B.

Prologue

Every part of my life as a writer seemed cursed. For example, creative inspiration always struck in the dead of night when I finally surrendered to sleep and my head fell wearily onto my pillow.

With eyes drooping, wishing to rest, I labored in front of my computer, soldiering on, and was rewarded when twenty-three hundred words miraculously appeared in my personal work in progress, a thriller that had held me hostage in a state of writer's block for weeks. Behind fatigued eyes, I was pleased with my progress and grinning like a maniac—mostly because of the twist I slipped in. The handsome new character I introduced several months ago—the one who happened to be based on my ex-fiancé—tragically tumbled off a cliff. *Ha, ha, so satisfying. Will he survive the fall?* I doubted it, because I left him alone on the ground as a puddle of blood pooled behind his big head.

I felt no remorse, only happiness. That character practically ruined my work in progress, turning it into more of a silly romance than a thriller, and the pleasure of sending the *Steve* character into a gorge made me giddy with delight. At least I could control something in my life.

The thrill energized me for yoga with Maxine and our guru, Adam. We always met on the back lawn exactly one hour after dawn.

Adam stared over the edge of the river bank, craning his neck toward the water for a better view. The neighbor's yellow Labrador bounced next to him, barking toward the water where a beaver built a dam earlier in the week.

Maxine rolled her eyes in irritation and continued stretching next to me. She abhorred tardiness, and our yoga session was already five minutes behind schedule. The old woman, my boss and landlord, kept a tight schedule on all of her activities. Her self-discipline was admirable but borderline obsessive.

"Isn't he cute?" I grinned at Adam, recalling the beaver chipping through branches while woodchips flew about. "Is he down there? Can you see him?"

Adam pursed his lips and turned extra wide eyes on me.

"I wouldn't exactly call him cute." He frowned back down at the embankment. "He's impaled and must have fallen directly on a sharp branch. Definitely dead."

"Oh no!"

I jumped to my feet and hurried toward him, but he held up a hand to stop me.

"You don't want to see it," he said.

"The beaver is dead?" I asked.

"Definitely dead, but not a beaver," he said simply. "It's a *body*."

Chapter 1

His golden eyes locked with mine, beautiful, intense, and hypnotic, and they gleamed with a slightly lighter hue in the late afternoon. He was a handsome specimen, powerful looking, a definite predator. Turning slightly, he flirted with me, twisting his head slowly under my admiration. He'd perched there before and noticed me plenty of times. We were very familiar and had grown accustomed to each other in the past months, searching for one another to admire. He knew I couldn't help watching him, because he always stole my undivided attention. So, he posed at different angles, ensuring I got a good look at him, well aware of my obsession.

He never allowed me to watch him flutter off. He always waited for the evening to grow too dark, or until I happened to glance away. He enjoyed the guessing game—was he still there, or was he not?

Definitely a little devil with those pointy ears, and exactly like my ex: handsome, commanding, alluring, and deceiving. Even so, I would miss him, my little owl friend, when I finally moved out of the guest house.

The big house, where my ex-boyfriend wandered, dwarfed my little bungalow. The mansion lay thirty steps north of my elevated porch, on higher ground. Earlier, Steve's silver Porsche had skidded into the driveway, and I hesitated going over there, resisting the expectation that I would hurry at his arrival. *Gad*, like that magnificent owl, he was easy on the eyes, and I found myself itching to see him. Dread shivered through my body at the thought of going into the big house and possibly caving in at the sight of him. My only hope was to avoid him, but I knew they were expecting me.

Lovely old Maxine lost her second son earlier in the week—Richard, a man who had disappointed her over and over again. Weak and frivolous, hiding in Brazil, *he's a sixty-three-year-old child*, she had spat, creating illegitimate children in every port and trying to ruin the family name. The opposite of her other son, Steve's father. He had been the light of her life, and her grandson Steve was the image of him in every way, shape, and form.

I did not want to see that particular grandson, but Maxine insisted I take the opportunity to finally meet all of her grandchildren. They were gathering at her river mansion to discuss the family trust fund. A fund slated to be disbursed within one year of the death of that second son, Richard. As the ghostwriter hired to pen parts of her memoir, she believed it critical for me to meet everyone. My animosity toward my ex-fiancé needed to be moved to the back burner. I couldn't let my personal feelings keep me from my professional duties.

Maxine owned seven acres right along the Sacramento River next to the Garden Highway. A wooden walkway linked the guest house with the main mansion. Because the river flooded yearly in the capital city, my structure was partially elevated to safeguard against the high winter river and stilted over lower ground, while the main structure was built on a higher area that was part of the levee system. A floating dock, beyond the high riverbank, was attached to a gangplank and fluctuated with the water level.

The little devil, a great horned owl, lived in one of the majestic old oak trees scattered between the house and river edge drop-off. His nest was well above the floor of manicured acreage, about eye level with my stilted porch. On a taller tree, closer to the river, a lone tire swing moved lazily in the soft breeze.

"Amanda!" Kira called from the mansion's side door, the one joined to the plank walkway leading to my back bedroom door. "Maxine is wondering where you are."

"I'm coming."

Damn, I did not want to look at Steve's face, but anything for Maxine. She was more than my employer, she was a dear friend and had pulled me so completely into her fold. I admired that old woman more than anyone and did not enjoy disappointing her.

No doubt she expected me to speak to her philandering grandson again and forgive him. Not a chance, at least not yet. Eleven months ago, when I agreed to spend one year in the guest cottage ghostwriting parts of her memoir, I hadn't realized her ulterior motive had been to set me up with her prized grandson. But she did, and it worked, and I fell unabashedly in love with Steve and his charming ways. I had even agreed to marry him less than a month ago, before discovering the real him. The philandering, predator him. My stomach tightened thinking about it, falling in love with my worst nightmare.

It took a very deep breath and a pile of courage to walk down the plank.

Self-pity welled in my gut. Less than a month ago, I had it all: a home, a friend, a mother figure, a romantic lover, an upstanding man, and the glorious possibility of having babies… But it turns out, that dream would forever stay a fantasy. So sorry to lose Maxine, and so sorry her memoir wasn't complete, but something deep in my gut knew Maxine was never really concerned about her memoir.

Kira, Maxine's nurse, sighed when I arrived at the door. She happened to be a petite, dark-haired, no-nonsense girl with small children at home—my exact opposite, except for the petite part. Maxine probably urged her to stay late to meet everyone, and Kira stayed out of politeness. If she could do it, so could I.

"Please make sure she checks her sugar before bed," Kira whispered. "She loaded the table with sweets, and your Steve brought her a white mocha from Starbucks. What is wrong with him?"

Everything, I didn't say, but tilted my head to give her peace of mind so she could leave easily.

We tramped down the dark hall where an assortment of voices bounced off the walls. Kira beelined to the front door, waving as she went. She had children at home and never stayed a minute longer than necessary. When I fully entered the gathering, my eyes gravitated directly toward *him.*

He wore his polo shirt stretched tight across his chest and his collar was open wide enough expose his thick muscular neck. He immediately ran a hand through his scruffy hair as our eyes locked. His eyes glowed with a hopeful expression. I smiled at the tinge of yellow circling his left eye, the one I had blackened last week. He bit his lower lip, all the while fluttering his dark lashes at me, and exactly like the devil in the oak tree, he pivoted slowly to give me a better view of his roughened square jaw.

A disgusted puff of air snorted out my nose in response because my stupid heart had actually lifted at the sight of his lovelorn face.

"Amanda!" Maxine beamed. "Come over here." She stretched a hand out to me.

Maxine was slender with a regal air, beautiful silver hair, clear blue eyes, and translucent skin, and she stood with confidence, completely unhunched by time. Anyone could sense the energy radiating from her. She was frail, but she had power. Her array of scarves flowed in dramatic silky color around her, and her lips were bright pink, like a teenager's.

"Everyone needs to meet Amanda, my ghostwriter and soon-to-be…" Maxine flickered her eyes between Steve and me. She noted my face and drew in an elaborate breath. She turned back to her small group of grandchildren. "Well, we'll settle everything soon enough."

Maxine waved a hand vaguely toward each person as she named them. The twins were both blond and blue-eyed, and I could see what she meant when she declared I resembled one of her grandchildren. Except, Aster coated her light eyes in thick black liner and wore a thin tank top, ripped jeans, and a chunk of metal around her neck. She glanced at me fleetingly from the other side of the room, barely interested.

Alex, her male twin, looked much older than his thirty years. He was paunchy, with long flowing bangs and a deep tan that made his pale eyes pop. The whites were riddled with red. Clearly, Maxine did not exaggerate when she had once claimed, *the illegitimate twins were, unfortunately, drug addicts.* Years back, she had wanted to disown them from the family, she confessed, but her late husband Henry wouldn't entertain any such notion. He drove that point home with the iron-clad trust he drew up.

"Nice to meet you," Alex nearly shouted across the room. "Can't wait to read the juicy parts of Grandma's memoir." He chuckled next to my ex-fiancé.

James, the only grandchild sired during a legal marriage from her second son, appeared polished in a neat sweatered outfit and a perfectly trimmed beard. He shot me a friendly smile, and there was something trustworthy about his eyes. I liked him instantly. He looked respectable and appeared slightly amused with his raunchy half-siblings.

"Hey there." He nodded at me. "I believe we may have spoken on the phone once or twice."

"Oh, yes, nice to finally meet you face to face."

We shook hands. James had a firm, warm grip.

Steve had mentioned James a few times, the only cousin he really talked to, but they were not buddy-buddy. They were nothing alike, Steve had asserted, which I now considered another reason to be partial toward James.

One more grandson was expected, another illegitimate child, but he was still in transit. He was the one who had called last week with the bad news. He was delivering his father's ashes from Brazil, along with a few personal items and a handwritten *Last Will and Testament.* He was due at the Sacramento Airport sometime later in the evening.

After the basic introductions, Maxine directed us to the dessert table. She insisted everyone sample the treats, and I watched her nibble on a chocolate eclair. I purposely kept Steve on the other side of the table, moving away from his every approach. The twins unknowingly helped by trying to chat him up. They diverted his attention, giving me ample time to move away.

Someone let out an amused chuckle. James was watching the chase from behind his clear-rimmed glasses. He stepped to my side, putting a buffer between myself and my ex. We smiled at each other.

"You're petite, not what I expected at all," he said. He avoided all of the treats, just holding a flute of champagne in his left hand. "Maxine raves about you. Said you reminded her of her. I can see what she means."

"Maxine is quite a lady." My eyes went to the older woman, who now nibbled on a thin serving of lemon cheesecake.

"How's the book coming?"

"We wrote close to fifty thousand words," I told him. "But honestly, she hasn't even gotten out of her teens yet and hardly ever wants to work on it."

He chuckled.

"Not to worry," I told him, "She says most of the middle ground is already written. My part is basically a rewrite anyway, to make sure she did justice to her younger self. I guess that's why she hired me. We both grew up in Boston and have similar places and experiences in common."

He continued nodding, watching Maxine.

"She's not supposed to consume so many sweets," I whispered. "The doctor recently put her on insulin shots. I'm not certain how to ensure she checks her blood sugar later."

His worried eyes met mine. "I'll take care of it. We can check our levels together," he whispered. "I'm familiar with her diagnosis, she called me when the shots were added. Maxine went into total denial when diabetes was added to her medical resume years ago and never follows any orders. It upsets her to follow instructions. Now, with the shots, she's probably upset all over again. When I stashed my emergency vial in the fridge, I saw that she's got a Mufolin pen, the Rolls Royce of insulin pens, not like the old needle and syringe we old hats sometimes do."

James is diabetic?

I didn't know much about James, or any of them. In the past year, Steve seemed to be her only living relative. She talked about the others sparingly, and I'd seen a few stray photos tucked into albums, but for the most part, they stayed away. Except, she did say James called once a week, and I caught her laughing on the phone with him on more than one occasion. I had even answered the phone when he called a time or two. She clearly enjoyed James, but when I inquired about him, she had closed her eyes and snorted.

"He's a nice boy, but a disappointment."

Suddenly, Steve reared up behind me, delivering "real drinks." He took the flute from James and delivered a tumbler of golden fluid. He offered a tall glass containing a vodka Collins, my favorite summer treat. I only accepted it because I needed something strong to propel me through the next hour, but accepting anything from Steve turned out to be a mistake. He grinned happily when I took it, which caused me to turn away, fuming for being cordial to him, always my first step to caving.

Aster pressed her forehead against the French glass patio doors, eyeing the large backyard. Her blond hair was pulled back in a messy bun, and her hands were opening and closing nervously. She appeared interested in the house next door, the rundown old mansion with a roof half covered by a blue tarp and overgrown vines snaking over the patio and creeping up the southern walls of the structure. The owner had planted an odd zigzagged garden of vegetables in the center of the yard and what he called his *girls* along the property edge. Certainly, more of those "girls" were indoors, but with the change in certain laws, he boldly planted them right along the border next to Maxine's pristine yard.

He was an awful neighbor and often lit small bonfires in his backyard. Everyone on our stretch of river believed he mooched off their electricity or other city services. I once caught him using Maxine's pool shower, and he often snaked long extension cords through the vegetation. We found his cords plugged into the outlet in the pool area more than once. Maxine hated him.

Aster gulped down her crystal of whisky in one go and turned her mascara-smudged eyes to Steve. "Does Chucky still live over there?"

Steve nodded and walked over to her. He poured them each another whisky. Alex joined them, and the three stood at the glass doors drinking whisky like it was iced tea and whispering together in hushed tones. The sunset glowed beautifully in the background with a pink sky framing the oak. Feeling more annoyed than ever, I found a place next to Maxine and plopped down on the cushions. She leaned over.

"They always make him drink like that," she whispered. "And he's upset about your little tiff. We should lure him over so you two can have a one-on-one."

Heat welled in my cheeks. Maxine was an assertive old woman, and from day one she pushed Steve on me. My first month in the cottage, she enticed him to visit day after day, insisting he take us out and about Northern California to wine country, the local music scene, and often begged out at the last minute. She pressed until we had started a relationship, and her ruse was no longer required. Her match-making plan had been obvious, but I initially found it amusing and didn't care. Steve was attractive, intelligent, an awesome date, and he turned out to be a skilled lover. I easily fell for his many charms.

"Amanda," she said. "You must allow him to explain himself. And you must keep your temper while he does it."

I shut my eyes. She chuckled.

"Oh, no worries, I've had to slap down a man or two in my day, and I admire you more for doing it. He needed it, he needs a strong woman like you, but boys will be boys after all, and any of that nonsense surely happened before you two really got going. You were learning things after the fact, I'm told, and as a handsome professor, what does anyone expect? And he's a literature professor at that, literature! Please don't carry this grudge any longer. He is absolutely heartbroken, as I am heartbroken. Two people, who obviously belong together, torn asunder by past circumstances. It's so heartbreaking. Amanda, this doesn't have to be a tragedy."

Did she have any clue to what I had discovered? Surely, she was not privy to the "toys" and the videotapes in that box; otherwise, he would no longer be the prized grandson. I was not going to be the one to tell her about his stash in the closet, it'd break her heart. Right now, she believed I was only upset about the long list of young lovers he had, mostly students of his, not his startling box of tricks.

James came around and sat on the other side of Maxine. He still nursed his tumbler of whisky, but the others remained at the window, emptying the bottle and laughing. James stared at them with a wary expression. Maxine reached out and squeezed James's hand, and he turned a weak smile on her.

"You okay, Max?" he asked softly.

"Don't worry about me." She patted his hand. "I forgot him a long time ago, after all that with your mother." She tutted at James. "Don't mourn him too much, James. Richard was a terrible father and doesn't deserve it."

I wasn't aware of all of the family gossip, but from the little Maxine shared, James had been abandoned by his father when only a baby.

A loud cackling laugh drew my attention to the window. Both twins stared directly at me, and Alex took a step in my direction. He actually pointed with his weather worn finger.

"She's the one?" His mouth pressed into a grin. "Why didn't you say so when she walked in?" Alex openly appraised me from head to toe. "So, you're the upset fiancé?" He chuckled, as did his twin sister.

He stepped closer, and I stiffened with a flash of fear as I glanced at my ex-fiancé. Steve's face melted into horror, and I could see his entire frame tense up. He obviously did not expect his drunk cousin to pounce after whatever he said.

"Did you really clock him?" Alex chuckled. "And throw the ring in his face. Good for you."

"Behave, Alex." Maxine's harsh voice cut through his giggles.

Steve gripped Alex's shoulder and pulled him back.

"I am behaving." Alex grinned at my face, before leering at the rest of me. "You must be a wild one if you tamed Steve-o. Let me guess, it was a whirlwind romance. He wowed you with his unbiased tongue, or was it the money?"

Steve physically pulled Alex several steps back, cursing under his breath. At the same time, James stood and slightly shielded me. Aster giggled softly, watching with her mascara-gobbed blue eyes. Behind her, Alex wriggled out of Steve's grip, and they exchanged a volley of angry huffed words. Maxine held my arm, keeping me from rising off the sofa. Everyone started talking at once, but all I heard was Maxine.

"Oh, those twins, they enjoy causing a stir. Ignore them," she hissed in my ear.

Steve's eyes flew toward me, sending a silent apology. His lips were pressed tight, and he appeared embarrassed.

"Don't mind my brother." Aster stopped giggling. She paused to watch how her grandmother hovered over me. Her eyes were unreadable, her voice a tiny bit raspy. "Everyone knows he's an asshole. Nobody likes him."

"I'm not as asshole, you little twerp," Alex shouted at her. He poked Steve's chest with a finger. "He's the asshole, isn't that right?" He seemed to have forgotten my name as he pointed at Steve. "Right?" he smirked toward Steve.

"Please behave yourselves," Maxine hissed again. "This is no way to act when we are gathered together on this somber occasion."

Alex released a long snort of air, and James stepped hesitantly forward.

"Oh no, don't you try sticking your nose in here, pretty boy." Alex gave him a menacing look. "We all know why Steve-o is set on marrying this girl." He pointed toward me with his thick finger again. "The *heir clause*. That's it, isn't it? Let me guess. You're a Mayflower Daughter, went to some fancy east coast school?"

What in the world is he talking about?

"Don't be ridiculous." Maxine gave him a glare. "I want you kids to try to play nice."

"Shut your trap." Steve shoved Alex against a chair.

Alex stumbled back, almost falling, yet he appeared amused.

"Afraid I'm going to spill your beans, Steve-o?" He stared gleefully at Steve. "I can take you down with one punch, old boy. You've gotten soft around the edges, haven't you?" He turned amused eyes on me. "Want to fulfill the clause with a real man, doll, just give me a little wink. I'm a much better linguist than Professor English here and might be open to trying out a new fiancé." He stuck his huge tongue out his mouth.

"You just stepped over the line." Steve shoved him again.

"Hey now, guys, not in front of Maxine," James said. "If you must have it out, take it outside."

"Yeah, are you afraid to take it outside with me?" Alex laughed. "Remember what happened last time we took it outside? Let's take it outside again, old boy. Are you afraid?"

"Take it outside!" James demanded.

Aster backed up a step, giggling at them. She opened the door for them, waiting.

Maxine appeared mortified. Her brow creased, and her head dropped onto her hand.

What in the world was the heir clause?

Alex suddenly flexed his fist, and Steve flinched, which made Alex laugh. Then, he threw out an air jab toward James. Alex grinned at me, and his red rimmed eyes actually twinkled. He was a complete ass, full of himself. His antics were causing Maxine to wheeze. Good lord, did he not remember his grandmother was nearly ninety? I fought an urge to go over and slap him because he appeared unhinged. *Is he on drugs?* Who knew what he was capable of? Alex and Steve exchanges a few more shoves and harsh words.

"Take it outside, please!" James boomed.

My arm hugged Maxine, and her body heaved with breaths. As Steve and Alex escaped to the patio, Aster chuckled and closed the glass door after them. James returned to the other side of Maxine, murmuring to her, while the two guys outside circled each other, throwing out random, ineffective jabs, all the while shouting out foul words and knocking over the patio furniture.

Inside, James helped Maxine stand. He gave me a weak smile.

"Sorry about all that. Those two have gone at it every time we've met." His voice was gentle. "Maxine and I are going to go check her levels and sort things out." He turned back to the old woman. "You probably shouldn't have finished that sweet coffee drink on top of the cake, Grandma."

Maxine nodded and leaned into James. They made their way gingerly out of the room. I was about to follow them when Aster let out a startled cry.

"Ooch!" she cringed.

Out on the patio, Alex bent over grasping his own neck with both hands, staring at Steve with bulging eyes. His entire face had gone red.

"Y-you tried to kill me," he stammered. "You maniac! A neck p-punch is a fatal move. Imma gonna c-call the police on you. I got a witness. You did that on purpose. You tried to kill me." He managed between choking coughs.

I moved closer for a better view and watched Steve tower over his cowering cousin, fists clenched. His chest was puffed out, and his arm muscles bulged as he flexed drawing in my attention. Steve was hot-hot-hot when he became emotional, and my pulse pepped up watching him strut about.

"If you say one more thing to her, I *will* kill you, you little fuck!" Steve spat out the words in a sharp, controlled voice. "Do you hear me? Stay away from her. You are not to look at her, speak to her, or think about her. You will keep your eyes and your fat tongue in your stupid head and be respectful. You hear me? You do not look at *my girl*."

Good lord, that comment hit me directly in the chest.

"I'm gonna report you. I'm gonna report everything."

"I'm going to kill you." Steve kicked him.

Steve's leg flew out to kick him again, but Alex spun off the deck onto the lower ground. He shouted several more profanities as he trotted toward Chucky's dark yard. Steve stood on the deck, shouting into the dark, flexing his fists and letting off some of his animal energy, quickening my pulse and my breath. When he turned around, his eyes locked right onto mine, fueled. Good lord, he made me dizzy.

But I pulled myself together and stomped away before I did something stupid.

Chapter 2

It was pitch black outside. Most nights along the river were calm and quiet, except for the sporadic hoot of an owl or two. Was the devil in the old oak mocking me, laughing at me for getting stirred up by my ex? *Weak and easy, that's me.* My eyes drifted toward the river mansion as the last of the lights went dim, signaling that the last one up had finally gone to bed. Steve's Porsche still sat in the drive, and I wondered where he was. There were five bedrooms in the mansion, which meant he would be going home to sleep, or finding a sofa. Surely, he'd never...

Distinct vibrations reverberated on the walkway between the mansion's back door and mine. Someone was walking over, someone with a familiar step. That buzzing sensation from hearing him defend me struck again. I sucked in a deep breath and went to meet him at my back door. Did he expect I'd talk to him? He was probably falling down drunk by now. I stood with crossed arms as he slowly strolled up.

"Hi." His voice was quiet. "You're awake."

He was surprisingly lucid and annoyingly handsome in the dark.

"What do you want?"

"I wanted to make sure you're okay," he said. "My cousin can be a bit much. I half expected him to try coming over here. He can be—"

"I'm fine," I cut him off. "And you know I can take care of myself. If your asshole cousin comes near me, he'll be sorry. You know my temper, and right now, I'm pretty angry. Just so you understand me, Steve, I am not planning to resurrect our relationship, so you should go."

He didn't move. He wore his wounded boy face, the one with his totally adorable puppy dog eyes.

"Can't we just talk?" He leaned against the railing, a little wobbly, drunk after all, but he hid it well. He spoke rapidly, "Let me explain. What you think you saw at my condo, what you think you found in that box, it wasn't anything like what you think it was. It's a pretend box of stuff. Pretend, Amanda, pretend. You know, workshop props for my students, aspiring writers, to try-out stuff they want to write about, feel things out. That's all it was, a props closet, to pretend, for exploring ideas."

I stood dumbfounded. Did he seriously expect me to believe him?

"Writers need to have first-hand experience, so wrestling out of zip-ties or handcuffs, if they're writing about it, it helps. It's a creative writing tool. Props to help. You happen to be a very talented, imaginative writer, but not everyone is. Some people need props and pretend situations to… you know, to get experience. To be able to write about stuff."

Now I let out an exasperated groan. "That's the lamest explanation I have ever heard. Do you really expect me to believe your load of crap?"

"Come on, Amanda, this is me." He held his hands out to his sides in surrender. "You know me. We've been together for nearly a year. You know I'm not some sexual deviant. If you want, you can ask a few of my students. They can—they can explain the process." His hand went up to rub his eyes. "I'm so tired I can barely manage a sentence here. Will you please let me explain everything in the morning? I'm in agony over here, and I love you, Amanda. I don't want to lose you over a simple misunderstanding. Promise me we'll talk in the morning."

Ugh! He made me feel like the bad guy. I clamped my teeth together. Finally, I nodded.

"Thangs." He blinked and chuckled at himself. He turned and looked a little lost as his wandering eyes met mine again. "I don't think I should go home? I don't wanna drive. Can I sleep here?"

"You definitely shouldn't drive, not in your condition, but you are not sleeping here. Try Maxine's big comfy couch in the living room," I suggested. "Or the one in the den. If you think I'm going to let you sleep with me, think again."

He flashed his classic grin, turned up on one side with a cheek dimple engaged, lopsided and amused. Truthfully, he was terribly attractive, and I loved his lips. His lazy eyelids fluttered in commiseration with his sad plight as he rubbed his jaw with a big hand. I hated that I watched every move with interest and that he noticed my interest, just like the devil. Eight long days had passed since we last made love, and having him stand there looking so eager, practically begging me with his eyes, made every nerve in my body a live wire. I could feel my resolve crumbling at the sight of his big hands.

"How about *your* couch," he said softly. "I don't want to be asleep in his path when he gets back. Alex is not known for being nice."

I was afraid to move an inch. He finally straightened and shook his head.

"It's okay. I'm not too bad. I think it'll be okay to drive. I'll go home. Don't worry about me, Amanda. I'm happy you've finally agreed to talk to me. At least I have that."

He turned and started shuffling slowly toward the house, not walking straight. Was he wobbling on purpose? The levy road was narrow, curvy, dangerous, and he always drove too fast. *Gad!* Was he trying to manipulate me? Ugh, my stupid heart. I was too easy.

"Steve, wait."

He stopped and turned those puppy dog eyes on me, which were my undoing. This was definite manipulation.

"You can sleep on the couch, but you stay on the couch, or I'll blacken the other eye."

He nodded and hurried back at a brisk pace. "Yes, yes, I stay on the couch."

It took more than an hour for Steve to fall asleep. The sounds he made echoed perfectly throughout the entire guest cottage because there was only one inside door, on the small toilet closet, and only half walls everywhere else. In the small living area, he kept shuffling around, making noises, sighing loudly. But I held my ground. I lay in bed statue still with my back to the living area and my eyes shut tight. Thank goodness, he never traipsed into the bedroom. I wasn't sure what would have happened, if I could have resisted him at close range. Spying on him strutting around the living room had really stirred me up. He had plopped onto the couch wearing very loose boxers and didn't use the cover I gave him. He was an awesome lover, attentive, giving, and very satisfying. Somewhere inside of me, I desperately wanted to believe all of his bullshit and drag him back into my bed and just relax, but I knew that would be a mistake.

His closet of toys with the videos on thumb drives was a hard pill to swallow. The things he filmed did not resemble a *pretend workshop* to me. It resembled the horror of a predator professor coercing young, insecure girls into doing things. I would know, because once upon a time, I had been a young, insecure girl myself. I hated him just thinking about it.

The small guest house suddenly became claustrophobic, and I needed fresh air. But going to the deck door was on the other side of the living room, and I did not want to walk near him—I wanted to escape. I pulled on flimsy slippers and snuck out the side door, which was attached to my bedroom. I tiptoed down the plank toward the main house and took the narrow walkway to the mansion's back patio where the steps took me down to the yard.

The night was moonless and totally dark. Though Maxine had commissioned the gardener to place accent lights along the property paths, they were rarely turned on. But I knew the grounds well and strolled out toward the oak with the owl. The river breeze stirred my hair and robe, cooling me, just what the doctor ordered to calm me down. Finally, I could breathe.

A single loud expletive pierced the silence, and I jumped.

Did it come from Chucky's yard? The way noise echoed off the levy walls, it could have come from either direction. The aroma of smoke from Chucky's firepit hung in the air, so I decided to find out what he was up to. He often stayed up all night and slept all day. More than once, I spied him roaming the grounds along the levy edge, always in the wee hours of the day. Sometimes he took a midnight dip in Maxine's pool. Maxine claimed it was his way of bathing and was infuriated when he used her pool uninvited. She recently had a security camera placed in the pool area with a plan to catch him in the act, but with everything happening the past month, no one had bothered to check any security footage.

"Just a little longer, and I'll get you your stuff," Chucky's raspy voice carried through the night.

Someone laughed huskily.

I meandered toward Chucky's yard, wondering who had laughed. He often entertained stray people around his firepit. As I drew closer, I could see flickers from the fire and heard interesting breathing sounds, like panting. I spotted them on the ground in the glow of the fire. Good lord, Chucky had a woman back there! They were going at it like animals, grunting and gasping, both completely naked, except for the leaves plastered on Chucky's back. They were smeared with dirt and foliage. It looked like they had been there a while doing these things on the ground. When she turned her head, I saw her face and got a shock. Good lord, that was Aster!

I immediately turned and walked rapidly back to the house. I never should have spied on Chucky. He was always entertaining in shocking ways so what did I expect? *Certainly not that!* It was usually only a couple of folks smoking a joint.

I took the pool route up to the back patio with a plan to go around the outer house, but a glance in the window told me someone was up and moving about. It was dark, but I'd recognize that man anywhere. Steve stood in the living room talking to James. Had he found my empty bed and gone looking for me again? The glass door opened easily, and I slipped right in, still a little shocked from what I'd recently witnessed.

"You are not going to believe what I saw next door," I whispered across the room.

Steve spun around, and I startled because the foyer man was not Steve.

Same size head, same height, same shoulders, same jaw line, same eye flutter, same head tilt and stance, but not Steve. This man was slightly trimmer, slightly straighter, slightly darker, and definitely younger than Steve. My brain became discombobulated, and my pulse skipped into a panic. I smacked my hand loudly on the thick table with enough force to make my eyes water.

"Oh, Amanda." Maxine came wandering in from the kitchen with a bottle of water. She offered it to the Steve look-a-like. "You're up again. Look who we found sitting on the front steps. This is Bruno, from Brazil. Isn't he handsome?"

The younger man blinked at me and nodded, clearly exhausted, but his eyes soon locked onto mine, and his brow twitched with a little worry. He glanced at my hand, and I hid it behind me, embarrassed. A whimper escaped my lips, and he appeared slightly concerned for me. He flashed a brief smile and tilted his head slightly. My heart instantly melted. He was completely adorable.

"Hello," I managed to squeak out.

"Bruno, this is Amanda. She lives in the guest house." Maxine beckoned James and Bruno to follow her down the hall. "Now, I want all of you kids to get a good sleep. James, I don't know why you're still up and about. I told you not to go walking near the property edge along the river. Please be careful out there, the drop-off can be startlingly deceptive. I won't be surprised if someone slips right over the edge someday."

"I was only on the porch making a call," James said. "The reception in the back bedroom is terrible."

The night had been so dark I had missed seeing James on the back porch when I walked by, was that possible? I wondered why Maxine never turned the track lights on. Did she keep the property dark on purpose, to discourage Chucky from wandering over?

"You too, Amanda," Maxine chastised me. "I know you are familiar with the grounds, but there are more and more vagrants lurking about. Chucky is inviting them over, I know it!"

"I never see any of them," I told her. "I think they stay on his side of the hedge."

"Don't be so sure. And don't forget, we have morning yoga with Adam, don't be late. We get our new routine. And Mister Daxter is coming in the afternoon, and afterward, we're going to dinner at the Firehouse in Old Town. We cannot miss dinner, not on my free night."

They continued down the west hall, and I stayed at the junction with Maxine. We watched the two men from a distance. Bruno completely entranced me with his near resemblance to Steve.

"James, please show Bruno to his room. He's right across from you." Maxine smiled at her two grandsons, watching as James pointed out the correct door for Bruno. "I'm so glad you made it safely, Bruno. We were beginning to worry about you. Good night, boys."

Bruno nodded and quietly thanked Maxine. He gave me another quick smile before disappearing into his room. James also grinned before going into his room. Maxine turned her bright eyes on me.

"He's at your place, isn't he?" she beamed. "No, don't say anything. I just want you to know I'm happy you're giving him a chance to set things right." Her cold, wrinkled hands covered mine.

I winced again.

"Oh, my, did you hurt yourself?" She glanced at my hand.

"It's nothing," I said.

"There's no such thing as a perfect man, Amanda, but that boy is about as close as you can get. I will die a happy woman if I can see him settle down with someone like you. Actually, exactly like you. We love you, Amanda. So, please, keep an open mind with him."

What could I say to the old woman? I patted her cold wrinkled hand before walking her toward her own bedroom. She wore her walking shoes. Like me, Maxine was a poor sleeper and often wandered around the grounds at night, sometimes going all the way down to one of the beaches to watch the water flow by. I wondered if she knew Aster was next door with Chucky. She must. She always seemed to know everything.

After leaving her, I slipped out the back door and onto the walkway connecting the houses, creeping as softly as possible down the plank.

Was I being too judgmental about Steve? Was I projecting my own stupid youth into the situation? Perhaps I should keep an open mind, as Maxine suggested. Maxine adored Steve, and she was not easily fooled. If I couldn't trust my own judgement, maybe I should trust hers. I certainly wanted to believe him. I slipped into my small bungalow and peeked into the living room to have a good look at him, but he was gone.

He wasn't in the bathroom, on the back patio, or anywhere in the bungalow. Steve had left. Where did he go? Maybe he woke up and drove back home, finally convinced he wasn't going to get anything from me. Somehow, that thought hurt my feelings. Oh, hang him! I was too exhausted to worry about it anyway and turned toward my bed.

Suddenly, inspiration hit, and every writer knew not to ignore the call of the keyboard. I changed course to my desk, and fired up the computer. The charming male character I added to my thriller, the love interest I spontaneously invented five months ago, needed to go. The words flew onto the page, thousands of words manically appearing. It would be a tragedy. It felt right, because that character needed to be eliminated from the story and a quick accident was the best solution without going back and changing all the work I'd done the past few months. Goodbye *Steve* character, have a nice fall from a fifty-foot cliff, perhaps he shouldn't have been hiking along the rough edges at night. So sorry you hit your head on a large rock. Good riddance to you, you sorry sack of shit. I punched out the final words before dawn. If I went to sleep right away, I could get two hours before Adam arrived for our morning yoga on the back lawn.

Chapter 3

Unfortunately, morning yoga was canceled because of a dead body.

Maxine, our yoga instructor Adam, and I stood six feet away from Shirley and her dog Rosie as the police secured the area, scoping out the scene. One of the officers had gone down the embankment attached to a rope to check things out. *Definitely dead,* he shouted up the levy wall. *Pierced through the torso after falling on a sharp branch,* the officer surmised. But who was it?

When Adam first announced the body, my heart plunged into my gut because Steve's car was still in the drive, and he had not been on my living room couch in the morning. I easily convinced myself that he had gone over the edge of the yard in a drunken haze looking for me. In the past, on more than one occasion, he had come searching for me during one of my nightly romps. Maybe this time he had stumbled over the levy. I thought about those words I wrote in the early morning. Could I have willed Steve over the edge with bad karma? *Please, no!* My heart raced with dread. *No,* Adam knew Steve well, and he would have said if it was Steve down that embankment.

Thinking of the devil, quite unexpectedly, Steve snuck up behind us. He poked his head between Maxine and me, wondering what was going on. I almost leaped into his arms, relieved he was alive and not like the character in my story, at the bottom of a fifty-foot cliff. I grabbed his hand, clutching it in my good hand, and stared into his eyes as a tidal wave of relief rushed over me. I was probably grinning like a total idiot.

"Good morning to you." His eyes slid over my face.

"Stop that," I whispered, throwing his hand back. "They found a dead body."

We stood stiffly apart, watching the paramedics. Steve reached down to reclaim my hand and noticed the bruised fingers when I flinched. He raised a brow at me. He inched closer and his presence instantly comforted me. My entire body missed him and ached with relief that he was okay. It took all my willpower to keep from slipping into his strong arms.

"It's probably a homeless person," Maxine mumbled. "More and more of them are wandering around, drawn to Chucky's yard. Maybe he's acquainted with this one."

But it wasn't a homeless person. When they pulled the body up, before they covered him, we got a glimpse of the surfer hair, the denim shorts, and the t-shirt. My insides flipped. Alex the asshole. I shot a look at Steve and caught his worried expression as he glanced back at me.

"Maxine…" he started.

"It's Alex," her eyes closed wearily. "It's Alex."

After packing off the body, a police officer made his way toward us. We congregated on the back porch of the main house, holding mugs of coffee and trying to settle our bearings. Steve kept staring at me with a funny expression on his face, which I ignored because I didn't know what it meant. James emerged from the house and slid into the chair next to Maxine. His bewildered eyes still appeared half asleep. Aster and Bruno were both still inside, unaware of the commotion. *Who's going to tell Aster her twin is dead?*

"Hi there, I'm officer Shane Bane." Officer Bane nodded to each of us. "I'm sorry about your loss. Anything you can relay about the deceased will be helpful in determining what happened. Were any of you up and about last night? Can you tell me what happened?"

"Alex and his sister arrived in the midafternoon," Maxine told him. "Alex became quite intoxicated, picking fights. If I were to guess, he slipped off the side of the levy in the dark."

"When did you last see him?" Officer Bane asked.

"When he stomped away at half past nine last night," Steve mumbled.

"Yes, at around that time," James agreed. "He ran over to Chucky's house."

Maxine and I nodded in agreement.

"Anyone have any idea if he came back inside or went anywhere else?" the officer asked.

"We were all asleep," James told him. "It was a very quiet night, at least for me, but you might want to question Chucky next door. He has given Alex drugs in the past, and perhaps that impaired him even more. I agree with Maxine, and would put my money on it, that he stumbled due to the dark and from being in an inebriated condition. I can't believe it. Alex is really gone?"

Officer Bane jotted everything down. He glanced at me with kind eyes. His voice turned gentle.

"How about you? Do you have anything to add?"

"Amanda and I were together last night," Steve quickly told the officer. "In the guesthouse, right over there" He pointed to the small bungalow on stilts. "We didn't hear or see anything. Your best bet is to speak with Chucky, as James said. Chucky's usually up all night, and Alex always goes over there when he visits."

I glared at Steve. I hated when he spoke for me as if I were a child. He saw my look and shrugged.

"Sorry," Steve amended. "I certainly didn't hear anything. Did you?"

"No, I didn't," I said stiffly.

Officer Bane closed his small notebook. He thanked us for our time and was sorry for our loss. He left a card with Maxine in case we had anything else to add.

As soon as he left, I excused myself and scurried away. My late night left me lethargic, and the family needed alone time. My anxiety had swelled to an all-time high, and I needed to escape to decompress. I felt guilty about the words I added to my work in progress the night before and wanted to delete them. The coincidence spooked me. Trying to kill off my MMC, the male main character, sat heavily in my chest, and I felt ironically at fault for the accident. Plus, I realized that my *Steve* character needed to resolve parts of the storyline, so he couldn't die yet, and I needed to think up a better solution than a sudden death. Unfortunately, I didn't know what to do with him. I sighed and fell into my classic writer's block remedy—hide from everyone and read a book, or take a nap.

Someone rapped sharply on the side door, the one attached to my bedroom and the plank walkway, interrupting my writer's block coma. One glance out the small window, and I spotted Steve. I opened the door and took in his fresh clothes, smooth cheeks, hands in pockets, and discouraged expression. Not flirty Steve. *Did he finally accept the demise of our relationship?* My fingers automatically raked through my mess of blond curls, a nervous habit, and my bruised and swollen knuckles caused a small gasp to escape my lips. Ice, instead of typing, would have been a smarter move. I waved him in.

"What is it?" I retreated from him and kept the bed between us. "I'm not ready to talk."

"Daxter is here," he said softly. "Maxine insists you sit in on our meeting."

Maxine rarely discussed her late husband in our sessions. Last week, when news of her last living son had passed away and the trust her husband had set up would now be dissolved, Maxine insisted I attend the Tuesday meeting with the lawyer. It would give me insight into Henry, she said, to listen in about the trust. Perhaps, it would paint a better picture of his controlling but caring attitude and open my eyes as to why she had stayed with him till the end. She always confused me with such statements. What did they mean?

"Oh God, is that still happening?"

He nodded.

"Even after this morning?"

"Maxine meets with Mister Daxter on Tuesday mornings, and you know how she is about routines," Steve said. "It'll be good to keep to her on a normal schedule. She's old."

"How is Aster?"

"She's… surprisingly okay."

"I'll come over in a minute." I stayed on my side of the bed, arms crossed. "Give me a chance to dress properly."

Everyone sat gloomily drinking at the dining room table. My eyes instantly landed on the young Steve look-a-like, Bruno, and he brightened at my glance. His resemblance to Steve was uncanny. It took a physical force to turn away, but then my eyes fell on the real Steve, who had noticed my eye-lock with his young cousin. I rolled my eyes, and they happened to land on Aster. She appeared drugged and lost, not sad, but annoyed and trapped, nursing a drink. Was it another whisky? I walked all the way around the table to sink into the seat next to James. He was the only person projecting any form of comfort to me. Coffee, cookies, and treats lined the center of the table.

Mister Daxter opened a folder full of papers at the head of the table. He wore an old-style suit with a vest. A handkerchief actually poked out of his breast pocket. His hair was on the long side, slicked back with hair grease, and he had a pencil-thin mustache on his upper lip. He appeared to have dropped out of a 1940s movie.

"The trust will officially dissolve between six months to a year from the official date of Richard's death. In lieu of any spousal claims, the estate will be equally divided among all eligible offspring of the two heirs of Henry Nathaniel Winters. This may require a liquidation of the meat packing assets and…"

I blanked out on the rest of the dribble, what did I care? I stirred two cubes of sugar into my coffee as my eyes flickered up and landed on Bruno again. He shot me a small smile, and I quickly averted my eyes, just to have them land on Steve. He sat next to Maxine, patting her hand with an air of concern. Maxine was watching me. She quickly sent me a small smile, which I returned, but at that moment, Steve moved his head, causing our eyes to meet. He certainly thought I was smiling at him because he beamed back at me. I tore my eyes away, frowning into my coffee cup when Mister Daxter unexpectedly said something that caught my attention.

He said something about the *heir clause*. I perked up and focused my attention on him.

"Is there something you need repeated?" he asked.

"No, no, I don't think so." I glanced at Maxine, at Steve, at James. The room suddenly tensed. My voice was small. "What is the heir clause?"

That got every person at the table to shift a bit. Steve and Maxine fidgeted in their seats, they were no longer holding hands, and Aster actually cracked a small scary smile. Bruno furrowed his brow, and James pinched his lips, embarrassed.

"Do we need to air this out?" Maxine asked sternly.

"I guess we don't, as it doesn't apply to anyone here." Daxter nodded to her. He turned amused eyes on me and tilted his head in my direction. "It's a funny little clause Henry added for his own amusement. It affects the disbursement of the assets if any of the offspring marries the wrong type of person. But no one is married yet, right? There's no need to worry about that clause. And I'm told that there are no longer any impending marriages to assess."

Maxine let out a long sigh.

"Henry wanted to control our fortune even after his death," she hissed. "Let's not muddy the discussion with items of no consequence."

Bruno got the group's attention with a loud clearing of the throat. He blinked at Maxine before turning toward Mister Daxter.

"Pappa left his own will. He did not wish his assets dispersed." Bruno leaned into the table. He spoke with a deep voice and slight accent, attractive. "He leaves a widow, a loyal wife of twenty-five years. His portion of any trust should go completely to my mother, his wife. His dying wish was for me to travel here and ensure his requests were given consideration."

"Yes, well, that might change things." Daxter blinked before glancing at Maxine and Steve. "But only if we can confirm this new information. Such as, confirm the legal date of his marriage. This document stamped two months ago isn't going to be valid."

"I brought two sets of papers. The stamped one and the original."

Daxter nodded vigorously. "And I will take a closer look at everything and have your documents checked and validated. But you must understand, this new

paperwork is a surprise. We need to authenticate and—
"

"Wait one minute," Aster suddenly spoke up. "If our shitbag father had a legal wife, a widow, the rest of us get nothing?"

"No, no." Daxter waved a calming hand at her. "The assets will be split. His wife, his legal wife, will receive half of the trust, and the other half will be split between confirmed, eligible offspring."

"And is he confirmed?" Aster gestured toward Bruno.

Every eye fell on Bruno.

"Not until the DNA test comes back." Mister Daxter flashed a grin at Bruno. "So, you'll need to provide a sample if you want to be considered..."

Bruno straightened in his seat. "I'm here for my mother." Every muscle in Bruno's neck flexed. *Wow.* "And my father. I need to ensure his wishes are given value."

Aster huffed.

"We don't need a DNA test for Bruno," Maxine told Mr. Daxter. "Bruno is a carbon copy of his grandfather, like Steve. There is no question about his heritage. He is my grandson." She smiled stiffly at Bruno.

It felt awkward, being in their family business, and I no longer cared if Maxine wanted me to listen in. I wasn't listening anyway, and those two look-a-like men across the table were distracting me. I picked up my cup of coffee and abruptly left the room. I went out to the back patio and found a chair facing the river.

Not one of them appeared upset in the least about the recent events. Not one seemed to care that Alex slipped off the levy last night, but my own nerves were still shaking.

The door squeaked, and James joined me on the patio.

"Aren't you afraid of missing something?"

He shook his head.

"I'm sorry, James. About your father and your... brother. Are you okay?"

He nodded slightly. "I never met my father, not after he left when I was a baby. I have no memory of him." He shrugged. "We must seem like a pretty heartless bunch in there, discussing an inheritance after the morning we've had. But we, Steve and I, only met Alex and Aster a few times at most, visiting here, so, it's sad that he's dead, but..."

I turned to the river.

"I'm sorry, that sounds very cold," he sighed, "but I tried for years to connect with him and Aster, and nothing. I'm upset, but I barely knew him, so it's hard to be—"

I patted his hand, and my face creased with the aching fingers. He glanced at my bruise but didn't say anything.

"It's okay, James. I don't know any of what happened. I've only writing the childhood years for Maxine, up until the day she married your grandfather, Henry. She hasn't talked about any of you or your backgrounds. I guess there's some complicated history that I know nothing about."

We sat in silence for a while.

"I grew up in boarding schools, felt like an orphan, so nobody told me anything about anything for years,"

James said softly. "Not until I grew up. Then, Maxine told me everything after Grandpa Henry died."

"I didn't know," I said.

"It is what it is. It's a sad story," he said. "My father left because my mother was diagnosed with cancer, and he couldn't face the complications. The way Maxine tells the story, he ran off to live with an exotic dancer who quickly gave birth to the twins, and he immediately left the country in shame. Although the company sends money to them, Alex and Aster are practically strangers to me. I've only ever met them a few times before this visit, and on every single visit, Alex has picked a fight with Steve or me. He was an aggressive man. I think he was abusive to Aster too. They didn't get along."

His eyes stared toward the river and the oak trees.

"My father abandoned us all. He spent time in Mexico, and Central America, and ended up in Brazil. He rarely called home and never called me. Just sent an occasional card. I expect the twins would say the same. Or they probably never heard anything from him. So, Maxine was right, he isn't one to cry over."

I covered his hand, and he shot me a weak smile. "I'm sorry. You don't have to tell me this. It's none of my business."

"Oh, but it is," he nodded. "You asked about the heir clause, and no one told you the complete truth. Grandpa wrote strict rules about what one should or should not do. He even drew up a list of requirements for acceptable spouses. Marrying the wrong person got you kicked out of the trust. I imagine it's why none of us have married yet, his strict guidelines."

He shot a look over his shoulder.

"But what Daxter didn't mention is the cherry-on-top part of the clause. The big prize. If one of us, or even two of us, finds a partner that meets all his prime requirements, they will receive the lion's share of everything, or everything, if a baby is in the making."

"What do you mean?

"Alex said it last night. Blueblood, Mayflower Daughter, college grad, but not just from any college. Grandpa drew up an interesting list. You speak French and German, right? Got those pretty blue eyes and natural blonde hair, all the Aryan characteristics. Let me see, there's more."

My cheeks began to heat recalling the questions Maxine asked when we first met: What college did I go to, when did I graduate, where was I from, who were my ancestors, did I dye my hair? Had she been scoping out the perfect mate for Steve?

"Bottom line, if you marry Steve, as things stand," James told me, "he will cash in on half of the trust, and if the two of you start a family, even only a confirmed pregnancy, Steve will get everything, assuming you check all the boxes, which I'm pretty sure you do. Maxine would love for Steve to be the sole trustee, or at least get half of everything. She's always favored him."

"Why would she want that?"

"She hated my father," James said. "She wanted to cut him off completely, including any of his children, like me."

He stared right into my eyes. What was he telling me? Could he be telling the truth?

He looked down. "She's changed her mind about it over the years. Accepts me now, and even the twins, but sometimes I get the feeling she'd like Steve to retain control of the company. He needs at least half of the trust for that."

We both jumped in our seats when the door opened. Steve's eyes narrowed at James as he joined us on the patio. His hand fell to my shoulder, and I shook it off. I stood and stepped away from him. He gave me his hurt boy face again.

James also stood and glanced between us.

"Daxter left, Maxine didn't want him at dinner. Our reservation for the Firehouse is in an hour." Steve raised his eyebrows at me. "Would you like to ride with me? We could talk in the car. Maybe get a little private time."

I shook my head and wrinkled my nose at him. How dare he pull his sad face on me.

"I'm not going to dinner."

Chapter 4

Of course, I was going to dinner, Maxine had insisted. She was an old woman, a creature of habit, and she never passed up a free meal. Because of her late husband's hefty, continuous donation to Old Town and the historic buildings, the Old Town collective gifted her with a free dinner at the Firehouse once a month on the third Tuesday. She could invite up to eight guests but rarely brought anyone besides me and Steve. For the past week, she excitedly gushed about the prospect of having a larger party at her monthly dinner. One that included more of her grandchildren.

I sat in the plush black leather interior of Steve's silver Porsche and stared out the tinted windows, angry at myself for not being able to say no to that old lady. The information James revealed rested heavily in my gut. I already knew she favored Steve over her other grandchildren. Did she want him to win the lion's share of the trust fund too?

Maxine and I had been friends for nearly a year. Our conversations had often ended in giggling sessions, and we had a true bond, a real sisterhood, a connection I'd never had with any woman before. My mother died early in my life, and my own grandmother never bothered to concern herself with me. Maxine had filled a vast void when she decided to embrace me. I looked up to her, wanted to be her and adored her. She was still sharp, had lived a glamorous and full life, and was her own woman. It wasn't rocket science, figuring out she hoped Steve and I would hit it off. She was not secretive about that. But now I wondered about her true motives. Did she want *me* for a granddaughter or my pedigree? I knew she hoped for a great-grandchild, and now I realized why she was so ecstatic about me and Steve. I was better than safe to marry in regards to his trust fund.

"Whatever James was feeding you on the patio, be careful believing it. He enjoys spinning up a web of lies."

I glanced at him. *James is the liar?* Yeah, right.

"He told me more about the heir clause."

Steve let out a laugh. He turned amused eyes on me.

"He's always been upset about that clause." Steve chuckled. "He's wanted to marry old what's his name for years but can't until he cashes in on his inheritance. Being gay is a definite no-no in the trust paperwork of Henry Winters. It totally violates the heir clause. He should cool down already. He has less than six months to wait. After which, he can marry anybody he wants."

Is James gay?

Now that it's out there, of course, he is. I kept my eyes fixed on the foliage passing by to keep from looking at Steve. Even though I was angry, he was still attractive and his musty cologne was beginning to affect me, reminding me that the best sex I'd ever had was with the man in the car. It was upsetting that he easily affected me on such a physical level. Steve loved taking the scenic route to Old Town, he often drove down the garden highway and looped around to the other side at the bridge, just to have a longer drive. I glanced at him.

"He mentioned a different part of the clause. He said if you married the right person, someone who fulfilled specific criteria your grandfather wrote out, that you'd obtain everything in the trust fund, or at least a larger part of everything."

Steve nodded, listening. "I'm not sure I know what you mean."

"Alex mentioned it last night when you were fighting. Mayflower Daughter, a degree from Wesseley, the right genetics, any other boxes to check? It sounds kind of racist. Is that why you wanted to marry me? Do I check off all the boxes in that clause? Does marrying me give you a more lucrative cut of the trust fund?"

Steve shook his head. His lips were pressed in a tense line.

"James is pulling your leg. There's nothing like that in the clause. The clause only cuts someone out of the trust for marrying the wrong type, you know, someone with a criminal record, or a history of mental illness, drug addiction, genetic diseases, and a history of… homosexuality. Grandpa may have been a bit of a bigot."

He looked me in the eye.

"James is sour because he hates seeing me happy. He can't marry the guy he loves, but I can marry you. He hates how nice you are and that Maxine loves you, and I love you, and you love me—at least, I hope you still love me," his voice cracked. "I want to marry you because I love you. I love *you*, Amanda. You're everything to me."

His eyes were wounded, glistening, and he gripped the steering wheel.

Those three little words slipped right into my chest to grab at my heart. Just a couple of weeks ago, I had been crazy happy in love with him. I had been flipping through bridal magazines and jotting down baby names.

"Please say I didn't blow it." He shook his head. "That box in the closet, I'm being honest with you, that stuff was part of a class project, a writing from experience project. I didn't come up with that exercise, the students came up with it. If you want, you can ask one or two of them, or all of them. They'll tell you it was a class project. It was stupid of me to participate in their games, but I'm a hands-on professor and love to interact with my class."

His puppy dog eyes blinked rapidly, and his chin trembled. He loved me, I was sure of it. And he smelled so nice, like a drug, and his hands were so large on that steering wheel. I very much wanted to believe him, so I nodded slightly, because deep down, I wanted to keep searching for baby names.

"Who should I ask?" I said softly.

He immediately pulled the car over and dug out his cell phone.

The Firehouse restaurant in Old Town Sacramento was in an old brick building with valet parking. Inside, the dining room was littered with elegant tables and large gaudy artwork. Giant chandeliers and waiters dressed in black waistcoats completed the aesthetic. We all merged around one large round table. They used real silver, crystal, and soft silky napkins, and the chairs were all heavy wood and cushioned in velvet. Maxine, James, Aster, and Bruno were already seated, sharing a bottle of wine. Anyone observing the table would never imagine a family member had been pulled dead from a beaver's dam that morning. I glanced at Bruno and saw that the line of his jaw appeared tight, clenched. His eyes were fixed on the crystal of water before him.

Bruno was not fond of his relatives.

Steve scooted his chair closer to mine, and I allowed his hand to caress mine. His happy face did not go unnoticed by Maxine, and she perked up with a twinkling smile. We exchanged slight nods, and I was happy that she was happy again. I turned to see James staring at me with a little tinge of concern. I did not know James, had only just met him, but I did know Maxine and Steve. They had been in my life for nearly a year, and it had been a good year, a loving year, the best year of my life if I was being honest. Maxine had been like the mother I had never known, a mentor and friend, and Steve had been the most fantastic boyfriend and lover. I adored Maxine and had fallen in love with her grandson. Over the years, she must have met hundreds of women that fit that crazy clause, but it was me that she introduced to her grandson, and me that he loved.

For the time being, I decided to believe Steve about his closet of props. It was his only red flag, and perhaps I had jumped to conclusions and seen things out of context. Two of his students had confirmed everything he told me. It was a class activity, and they, the students, had begged their professor to participate.

The only red flag until his cousins showed up, flashed in my mind. No wonder he kept them at a distance.

The absolute truth was, I missed him. The kiss we exchanged by the valet parking sign set my nerves on fire, and I was eager for dinner to be over so we could disappear into the bungalow and make-up properly. A tumble in bed was what we needed. I didn't agree to put the ring back on, but that was probably going to happen before the end of the night. I did not officially agree to anything yet, but my response to his kiss let him know where things were headed. I had desperately been feeling the withdrawals all week and knew half of my upset attitude revolved around my frustrated desires. Call me weak, but sometimes I needed what I needed, and apparently, I needed Steve.

The conversation around the table centered around Maxine as she told stories about her late sons. When they were boys, they were smart young gentlemen with an affinity for sports. She felt certain the move to California steered her younger son to darker influences. But in the end, she realized, they were both a blessing. And her grandchildren were also blessings, all of them, she insisted. Maxine went around the table to give each of them a compliment; Steve, James, Aster, and Bruno. She paused, suddenly silent, probably thinking about Alex.

"We should always remember those who have passed." She closed her eyes.

We froze as a heavy cloud descended on the table. The only one who kept moving was Aster. She picked up her water glass and drained it in less than a minute before slamming it back down on the table. The motion got Maxine to open her eyes.

"Don't forget your fathers," Maxine smiled weakly. "And also your mothers. Let's not forget the women who gave me grandchildren."

She smiled at James.

"Your mother was a ray of sunshine, James. Everyone loved Lily."

James grunted and gave a quick nod.

"Your mother, too, Steve. I loved Christine with all my heart. Both your mothers were true ladies. Knew the correct order of things. Love, marriage, followed by children."

Steve nodded.

"Both my sons married exceptional women."

Good lord, someone needed to steer the conversation. Did she not notice Aster beginning to bristle? Was she unaware of Bruno glaring in her direction? Both Steve and James glanced around nervously. Thank goodness the waiter interrupted with the water pitcher. Maxine flirted at him, then her eyes popped open as she admired the people at the next table. One of the men looked slightly familiar.

"Officer Bane?" Maxine exclaimed.

Everyone from both tables stood to greet each other. Maxine introduced Bruno and Aster to the police officer, and Shane Bane nodded and smiled pleasantly, but his eyes were stretched wide. Was he surprised to see us all out to dinner? He offered condolences before introducing his dinner companions. An older couple, Bob and Joanne, who had been dog sitting for him, and also his girlfriend, Sarah.

"You're a pharmacist? May I ask you a few questions? My doctor is pushing a new medication at me, and I never asked how it might affect some of my other pills." Maxine pulled Sarah off to the side for a private chat.

The rest of the crowd closed the circle around Shane Bane and asked about police procedure and what was expected next in the investigation of Alex's fall. Aster immediately wandered off, and my heart felt terrible for her. Those men, especially Steve, could be very thick-skulled. Perhaps they shouldn't refer to her twin as *the body* in front of her. I retrieved my hand from that idiot's grasp and hurried after Aster.

She zigzagged quickly around the hall linking the main dining room to the back bar. She did not dive into the lady's room as expected but swiftly escaped into the back room instead. The room was practically deserted, with only the bartender and one old man reading a book at the end of the bar. I caught up just as she ordered a rather stiff drink and settled on a round red stool. She noticed me, and her face instantly altered into annoyance.

"Sorry, am I intruding?" I paused. "I only wanted to check on you."

"I'm fine," she snapped sternly.

"I'm so sorry you had to hear them speaking like that. It's extremely insensitive."

"They're all dicks."

Aster grabbed her drink and gulped down a fair amount. She wiped her lips with the back of her hand and continued to stare with a bit of hostility. I inched away, not sure what to do. She was obviously hurting, but scary as heck.

"So, I can see that you're going to jump right back on board with that shit show called Steve." She scoffed. "I thought you wizened up, but no."

She shook her head and started rummaging through her purse. She shot a hostile look at the bartender.

"Is anyone going to get their panties in a wad if I do a little line over here?"

The bartender gave her a stern look.

"Fine." She pulled out a mint tin and treated it like a maraca. She grinned at me, then opened it up and popped one in her mouth. She held the tin up to me. "Go on, they won't hurt you. They're so mild I have to pop two or three to feel anything. They're great for helping us girls live with the evil choices we make."

It looked like an innocent mint tin, and I was at a complete loss for words. She laughed at me loudly. After a moment, she snapped the tin shut and dropped it into her purse.

"What'd he do?" She looked me up and down. "To piss you off. Let me guess, you caught him with a cute young thing, and you punched him. Did he try to convince you it was a one-off?" She took another taste of her drink. "They all say that, honey."

She was absolutely hideous. Her twin brother died less than twenty-four hours ago and she was amusing herself with drugs, alcohol, and taunting me. Maxine had not been exaggerating when she described this woman. I frowned and turned to remove myself from the situation.

"No, that's not it. Your type expects him to cheat." Aster fidgeted with her crystal tumbler. She pulled the small bowl of bar pretzels closer. "He's not a true man if he's not screwing around, right?" She laughed. "Wait a minute, did he ask you to play one of his *pretend* games? Did he get too rough? Was it beneath your lady-like sensibilities?"

The life drained out of my limbs, and I wobbled. Aster cackled at my expression.

"That's it!" She slapped her hand on the bar. "He should have known a prim and proper girl like you couldn't handle S&M games." She popped a pretzel in her mouth. "Give it another try, sweet thing. His games are extremely fun, you might surprise yourself. Steve-o is a complete dickhead, but he's good at the games."

"I… you-you're…" I was sputtering. "He's your cousin!"

She nodded, grinning at my horror. She retrieved her tin and shook it around again, chuckling.

"Who says cousins can't play games together?"

I was petrified to the spot, afraid to move, not sure if I could even breathe. Aster set the mint tin down on the bar hard enough for it to clatter. Her amusement dissipated in a blink of an eye, replaced by disappointment. She suddenly looked sad and disgusted.

"God, you are freaking easy, too easy. No wonder he likes you. Of course you'd think the worst." She turned her back on me and called for another drink.

My limbs became usable again, and they gingerly carried me toward the door. That exchange did not go anywhere near what I expected. The further I got from her, the faster I moved. Steve and James were still chatting with Officer Bane, and Maxine was still speaking to Sarah the pharmacist. *Aster knows about the*

S&M toys. It could only mean that Steve lied. It wasn't a foolish exercise with his current class if it went back far enough for Aster to know about it. Good lord, could she have actually participated in *games* with him? My mind unwillingly flashed to Aster and Chucky in the dirt the previous night.

For a few moments, I watched my handsome fiancé. *Did Steve ask those girls to sit by their phones waiting to lie to me?* His handsome face nodded at the police officer, and my stomach turned.

My feet shifted and took me straight for the door. I could not go back to that table. Even if *the worst* did not happen, he lied to me and continued lying to me, and he got those girls on the phone to lie to me. It made me nauseous knowing I had planned to take him home later. Why did I always fall for the monster?

Outside, I could breathe again. A streetlamp lit up the wooden walkway, and I turned toward the tower bridge but hesitated. The Steve look-a-like, Bruno, stood against the wall smoking a cigarette. He noticed me and straightened up, eyes opening wide like he had been caught being naughty.

Nope. I turned right around and quickly walked away. My footsteps fell so heavy they shook the wooden planks, but I did not slow down until I rounded the corner on K Street and made it as far as *The Garden of Enchantment* gift shop. I slowed but continued making my way to the end of K Street, crossed the cobblestone road, and strolled along the river. The air was finally breathable again, and the night along the water was dark, so no one could see my tear-stained face. That's when I noticed Bruno right behind me.

Bruno didn't just resemble Steve in structure, he also moved like Steve. They shared a similar gait, head tilt, smile, and even puppy dog eyes. But there was something in those eyes that were all his own. Bruno's eyes were innocent, but the rest of him was all Steve. I felt just as angry at Bruno as I was at Steve, and I glared at him. How dare he follow me! He needed to stay several feet away because I was ready to lash out at someone. He paused, surprised at my hostility.

"Why are you following me?"

He shrugged and sank fisted hands into his pockets. I immediately felt bad for glaring at him, and my rage ebbed. He wasn't Steve. He was an innocent bystander who had dropped into our world because his father recently died. Plus, he was much prettier, younger, and more defined around the edges than that maggot at the Firehouse, and he'd probably never be as easy a liar as Steve.

I shrugged back at him and took a few slow steps down the river walkway.

"I'm sorry for being unfriendly, but I'm extremely angry at Steve and…"

He hurried and quietly fell into step beside me.

"We recently broke up."

He nodded.

"It's been hard because it's a fresh breakup. I needed to get away from him for a bit, and to tell the truth, after this morning, I'm not sure how anyone can eat."

"I wanted to escape too," he said softly.

We walked down the planks toward J Street and veered toward the museums. We passed several folks on our stroll, mostly couples, and everyone seemed in a romantic mood. Bruno didn't say a word, he only smiled whenever I glanced his way.

My phone pinged a couple of times, Steve calling and texting. I quickly texted back, telling him I went for a walk and wasn't hungry.

At one point, the spiky heel of my shoe got caught in the plank walkway, probably due to my determined pace, and I nearly stumbled. Bruno caught me quickly, and an instant charge jolted me awake. It felt as if an electric circuit closed the moment his hand touched my bare arm. He flinched, just as surprised, and we both froze. He recovered and hurried back a few feet to fetch my shoe. Then, bending down as if I was Cinderella, he put my shoe back on my foot. That electric tingle flowed through my arteries again, and I found myself holding my breath. He stood up and smiled pleasantly at me.

"Thank you," I said stiffly.

"Yes, you are welcome. My pleasure."

What did that mean?

We continued down the walkway at a much slower pace, in a lighter mood. Bruno put his hands back in his pockets and kept glancing at my feet. Did he worry I'd lose that shoe again? Soon, we found an empty bench and sat down. All my anger had dissipated. Bruno pulled out a pack of cigarettes and offered one to me. I took it because it seemed like the right thing to do. Bruno produced a fancy lighter. He held the flame as I somehow got the thing lit. I coughed a bit, but he just flashed his small smile. He also lit a cigarette, and for a moment, we sat smoking in silence.

"Does everyone in Brazil smoke?" I asked.

His eyes were wide and surprised. He chuckled and sheepishly studied his cigarette.

"No, truthfully, I do not smoke. I was nervous with everyone and needed to be alone, away from them. So, I bought these cigarettes and lighter at the restaurant to give me an excuse to go outside," he confessed. "Do you often smoke?"

"I never smoke," I told him.

We erupted into giggles. We snubbed out our cigarettes, and he took them to toss into a nearby trash can. We couldn't stop giggling when our eyes met. It was so easy being with Bruno; the air was much lighter and bearable. I found some gum in my purse, and we each chewed a piece to get the smoky taste of nicotine out of our mouths.

He was incredibly handsome, turning the head of several passing women, just like Steve. But his eyes were definitely his own. They were more open, friendly, and amused, but with a different amusement than Steve's.

"Maybe, you will find a way to come back together?" His accent was cute and optimistic.

"No, never. I'm not…" I shook my head.

He nodded.

We chatted about Old Town Sacramento. I told him the little I knew about the historic flooding, the raised streets, the hidden first levels, and the old west. He hung on my every word and made me feel clever. I was actually smiling and laughing with him. He shared a funny story about jumping on trains in Brazil with his friends when he was a teen. They had skipped school and decided to jump a train to get to the next town. Turned out, the train was done for the day, and they ended up at the main station, so there they were, trying to hide and escape without being seen. They thought they were successful, but one of his friends had a father who worked at the station and told them that all the old men were watching and laughing the entire time they were sneaking around.

Did he get in trouble at home?

Yes, of course, his father gave him a long speech about responsibility.

I never laughed so much, so easily. He had lifted my mood effortlessly with small talk.

My phone pinged with another text, bringing me back down. Steve was worried. He wanted to know what had happened in the back bar. He wondered if Bruno was with me. Bruno stared at the phone, leaned back, and looked away from me, at the river. I quickly hit the call button.

"Stop texting me, I'm fine. I don't want to talk to you right now."

"Amanda!" His voice had an element of panic in it. "Aster told me what she said to you. My God, she was only kidding. She has a terrible sense of humor, and she's distraught about everything. She doesn't always choose the appropriate response. Look, honey, I told her why you were angry at me last night, right after you went to bed, about the props you found and the conclusions you jumped to, and Aster found it extremely amusing for some reason. She enjoys taunting people, and she's not thinking straight and..."

"Just leave it!" I hissed into the phone. "I don't want to talk to you right now. Please, just give me some space and stop trying to gaslight me."

There was a long pause. I could hear Maxine in the background saying something to someone.

"I'll have them pack up your dinner," his voice was soft. "Shall I come to find you with the car in a bit?"

"I'm not going to get into a car with you," I told him. "Why don't you give Maxine a ride home, or better yet, drive Aster. I'll ride in the Benz with anyone else. Tell James we're in front of the Railroad Museum when everyone is ready. Or better yet, maybe I'll get an Uber"

"Amanda…"

"Please don't drive over here. Please just give me space. If I see you right now, I will go ballistic."

"Okay, but don't call an Uber. Let James drive you home."

They were playing croquet on the back lawn, Aster, Steve, James, and Bruno, and they were drinking. Someone turned on the flood lights and much of the main plateau was lit up. The devil's oak was right in the center of the game, and they made that tree a middle stake for their balls to tap. Earlier, someone had knocked on my door, trying to get me to come out. I ignored him. They obviously believed I went to sleep. My bungalow was dark and quiet. I hunched into a dark corner on my balcony, watching them. Their voices carried over the air, and I could hear almost everything.

Steve strolled around with his mallet in one hand and a beer in the other. He appeared to swing that thing haphazardly, but his ball always went right where he wanted it to go. He was that annoying. He glanced toward me, and for a brief moment, it looked like he might be able to see me, but, no, he turned his head away.

"Left hand, left hand," James chided him.

"Oops." Steve chuckled in an intoxicated way.

"Hurry up." Aster's voice broke through. She stood in the shadow of a tree, so I couldn't see her well. Good Lord, did she completely forget that poor Alex was dead?

"Is it my turn?" Bruno lined up his mallet with a ball. He was the only one not carrying a bottle of something. "Shall I go to the tree or the little hoop?"

"Go for the hoop," Aster said.

"Go for the tree," James cut in. "Don't listen to her. She wants to knock you out."

Steve was staring at my door again. I don't know why his attention got to me in places I didn't want it to. I was a weak and stupid girl. I hated myself for still wanting to believe him. My brain kept telling me *NO*, but something in my chest was a prime idiot.

"Will you stop looking up there?" Aster came out of the shadows and stood right in front of him. "Just accept it. She doesn't want to marry you anymore, so you can put that plan to rest."

Steve said something I didn't quite catch, and Bruno stepped closer to them. I watched Steve turn to Bruno.

"What'd she say to you?"

Bruno shrugged his shoulders. "She spoke about the history of Sacramento."

James hit a ball, then walked toward the small group. He paused to knock someone's ball into the darkness.

"Just stop it with the rushed nuptials, or I might get nasty," Aster hissed at Steve. "In case you didn't know, Chucky has an Ivy League degree. If anyone looks super close, he pretty much checks off every box in Grandpa's grand plan. I can play any game any of you guys play, and better. So, just back off that idea. Leave it alone."

There were a few heated words I couldn't quite hear, and I watched Bruno take a few steps away from the crowd. He stepped behind the tree, and I couldn't see him. The three of them watched him and all faced him together.

"I'm following my father's wishes." I heard him say in a firm voice.

Bruno walked briskly to the big house. He went up the steps quickly, and I heard the outer door close. The other three watched his entire retreat as a united front. James scratched his head and turned to his cousins.

"I caught him rummaging through Maxine's China cabinet," James told them. "He claimed to be searching for a spoon, but when I took him to the kitchen, he just gave me an absent look. Do you think he's stealing things?"

They chatted on like that for a few moments. Bruno had been snooping around odd places.

Aster spontaneously threw her mallet on the ground and backed away from Steve and James.

"I have a date with my potential fiancé," she taunted. "I never got my resupply."

The other two watched her walk off, then James turned on Steve.

"Look at what you started," James said. "First, Alex and that woman he dug up, and now Aster."

"I don't know what you're talking about. All I did was get engaged." Steve waved his hand toward my bungalow. "This is a true engagement, or at least it was. It's not some game or ploy to beat anyone out of anything. Can't a guy fall in love? What I have with Amanda is not like what Alex was trying to sell." Steve pointed at my porch. "I love that woman! This has never happened to me before. I am truly, truly in love, and you people had better not ruin this for me!"

Good lord, my poor heart! Could it take any more yoyoing? He meant that, didn't he? I felt my head might explode. He loved me. My pulse was racing. *Don't think the worst.*

"You are going to beat me out of what's mine if you push it, right? I know Maxine is pressing you, thinks she is going to die without a great-grandchild, but this is so unfair to me, rushing things. We had an agreement! I can't do what the rest of you are doing. You're all trying to cut me out of what's mine."

"Unfair to you?" Steve gave James a little push. "This whole business is unfair to me! I should get half of that trust, hands down, without getting married or anything. I'm the sole son of my father, the one looking after Maxine! All the rest of you should be splitting the other half, or maybe the kid is right. That half should go to his mother, your father's wife. Maxine and I agree, the trust should be a fifty-fifty split. Any other way hoses me."

The scoff James let out carried loud across the yard.

"Taking care of her? I'm the one managing things. All you do is take her to dinner once in a while. If it wasn't for your fiancé, you'd barely be over here at all."

They continued bickering as they piled the mallets against the oak tree. Steve turned toward my place again, and for a brief moment, he seemed to lean toward finding his way to my stairs. But James had a hand on his arm and pulled him toward the big house. That was probably for the best. My heart and head were waging a battle, and I wasn't ready to decide what to do. I was still angry, but hearing his drunken declaration of love had touched me.

"Give her some space," I heard James say. Everything else was too mumbled to understand.

They walked up the mansion's back steps. A moment later, all the lights went out, then I heard the door close. A loud whoosh flew over my head as the owl swooped toward his tree. He wasn't visible in the dark, but I knew he was there, watching me. Had he been waiting for them to complete the game and turn out the lights? I stayed quiet for a few more minutes before going inside to find my own bed.

Don't think the worst, I told myself, heart pounding.

Chapter 5

The day was destined to be a lovely one, sunny and not too hot. My hand no longer ached, and I got a good night's rest, and despite all the nonsense, he loved me. It reverberated in the back of my mind, *he loved me*. He said that without prompting, with no agenda, so I could believe him, right? We had something good, got along, were physically suited to one another, and his grandmother adored me. *Who better would I find?* I was thirty-three, unmarried, and losing viable eggs with every passing month. I was lucky, right? A tall good-looking man with a job and stability, and he was fun, charming, had good taste, and—he loved me.

I grabbed my small recorder. Maxine always gave me tidbits of information for her memoir during our morning yoga session. We needed to work on that memoir.

Before going down to the yard for stretches, a quick peek at the front drive told me Steve's car was still out there. He had stayed at the house! That meant he hoped to talk this morning, which was something my libido wanted. Aster was right. I always lapsed into the negative, based on my unfortunate past, and I needed to work on trust, trust, trust. I needed to trust him, then maybe our love could come flowing back. Not just our pesty attraction, but the true love that drained out of me after seeing the contents of his secret closet.

Gad-dang-it! Just thinking about the snippet of video I watched put an instant cloud over my head, and I hated him all over again. One second, primed to take him back, the next, ready to toss him away.

Maxine was already up, out on the lawn, and rocking her tiger-striped leotard. She wasn't alone, as someone tall, dark, and handsome stretched next to her. My heart almost did a summersault thinking Steve woke early for yoga—something he'd never done before, though I've often begged him to join. A second glance told me it was Bruno. Bruno stood next to Maxine in a tight tee and small orange shorts, like someone from an eighties TV show, and my mouth went dry staring at his taunt muscles. *Had Steve been built like that once upon a time?*

"Look who decided to join us," Maxine exclaimed. She wore thin leather gloves again, not unusual in the morning. Her old delicate hands often got cold in the grass. "Everyone else is sleeping."

Bruno smiled brightly and lifted a hand, which set his chest to flex, causing me to quickly glance away. He had Steve's body, but worked and sculpted into youthful perfection, and I wondered if all of him was like Steve, if the endowment extended to a more private appendage. My face instantly flushed with shame at my own dirty mind, and I hoped nobody noticed.

"Is it acceptable," Bruno asked quickly, "Joining you?" He apparently noticed my flush face.

"It's no problem. As long as it's okay with Maxine." I kept my eyes off him.

"Oh, just put that away for now. Maybe we can catch up later on that stuff." Maxine pointed to the recorder. "I thought we'd just stick to yoga now that we've got a third. We can continue last week's routine."

We began with standing stretches, and Maxine led. She loved being the "yoga leader" when Adam wasn't around. Bruno followed along without much comment. He proved to be limber, even with the muscles, and he had a good range of motion. His orange shorts were an eye-catching color and strained over his hard tight tush and that hidden appendage, which pulled at my eyeballs like a magnet. I felt my face burning, lost my balance, and fell on my face. The embarrassment!

Bruno grinned at me and offered me a hand up. I ignored his offer and turned toward the river, wondering what was wrong with me. Was it his striking resemblance to Steve? Or maybe his totally cute smile? Or perhaps my body felt the acute withdrawals of breaking it off with my fiancé? Up until a week ago, our sex life had been very active. Whatever it was, Bruno's presence succeeded in turning areas of my body into a hot mess. Good lord, he was at least ten years younger, maybe more, but yoga movements from Bruno got me instantly hot. His body was basically a younger, more ripped version of Steve, and I always thought Steve's body was perfection. Until seeing what it could be. My rebellious mind kept imagining Bruno in passionate situations, and he didn't help matters by flashing his bright eyes at me every few minutes. He likely considered me a funny older woman.

"Amanda, breathe!" Maxine chuckled at me. "You are extremely red, and we haven't even gone to second stage yet. What is wrong with you today?"

Bruna stopped stretching and stood still. *Oh God, he noticed my ogling.*

That look in his eye. He knew my crimson face had something to do with him, and now I could feel myself turning even redder. Bruno took a tiny step backward, and his lips twitched at the edges. Did he find it amusing to have an older woman leer at him?

"Thank you for the stretching." He nodded at each of us. "But I will go run for exercise. Perhaps you will be more comfortable."

His eyes locked onto mine for a moment, and I swore they were saying something. I felt like such a cheater maintaining eye contact, but I couldn't move my eyes away. He finally turned and sprinted toward the steep drive on my side of the property. My pulse raced wondering what had been in his mind. Had he been thinking similar thoughts?

Maxine and I rearranged ourselves for sitting stretches, and I was happy those forearms and orange shorts were not around to distract me anymore. *What am I, a teenager?*

"Oh well, since he left, we can finish our last discussion on the wedding chapter. That is the first turning point in the memoir and needs careful construction. It is a focal point, and I decided to add in a few hard topics I left out of the first draft."

My head bobbed as I reached over and turned on my recorder.

We already covered her teen years, up to her wedding to Henry Winters. Those pages were written and waiting for edits. Now, Maxine wanted to reserve an entire chapter for her wedding, the wedding night, and the honeymoon. She met Henry Winters at the tender age of sixteen but didn't marry him until she was eighteen. When they met, Henry Winters had been a twenty-nine-year-old widower, an up-and-coming money-man in her fathers' business. He had lost his first wife in childbirth at twenty-four, and it took him a few years to get over the death of his wife and stillborn child. Maxine developed a crush on him the moment she met him.

"It was a different world, Amanda," Maxine said. "Don't get me wrong, I applaud you for standing up and letting your grievances be known, but believe me when I insist that Steve is about the most charming man around. Yes, he's my grandson and I'm partial to him, but I also know a good thing when I see it. Henry had his bad points, too, but if you weigh the good with the bad, he comes out on top, and Steve is just like his grandfather. He comes out on top. The cream of the crop."

She tsked at my scowling face. Should she be told about the closet of toys? The video of Steve *play-acting* in that way with that very young college student?

"Actually, he's a better man than Henry was, much better. He doesn't rush you, does he? He's patient, and he would never press himself on a woman. Tell the truth, he didn't even kiss you until you asked him to, admit it. He's a gentleman, and a modern man, but still a man.

Hard to do in today's society where these extreme feminists expect men to go against their natural nature."

Sometimes Maxine made surprisingly outdated statements.

"You don't understand why I'm angry," I said.

"You're upset at his behavior with those college girls," she responded.

"You know about it?"

"Of course," she nodded. "He's brought many of them around for dinner over the years. He's a good-looking man, a catch, so of course young girls are going to throw themselves at him. What do you expect from a virile man? But he never took any of them seriously, he was waiting for a real lady, like you. A proper, well-bred, well-educated woman from good stock. Somebody to settle down and make children with. You can't blame him for having a past, Amanda, and I imagine Steve was not your first dalliance. If it's the number of past women you're upset about, men have urges."

"I understand that men have urges," I snapped back. "But he is a professor, and they are his students. There is a power imbalance in the situation. Doesn't that bother you at all?"

"Those girls made a choice, they are not innocents. Why blame him for their misguided behavior, for throwing themselves at him? Really, Amanda, with men and women, there has always been a power imbalance. It's the natural state of things. Men hold the upper cards at the beginning of every relationship, but stick around long enough, and you'll hold the winning hand in the end, if you play your cards right. Once a woman gives in to a man's base urges, she can turn the tide in her favor.

She can have him in the palm of her hand. Don't be like me and learn that lesson the hard way."

I moved to stand, but she held me down with a hand on my arm.

"Don't fall for the misguided chatter of today's society, the whining. If I measured my relationship by today's standards, most would say that Henry raped a child, and I should have left him or some nonsense of the sort. My goodness, today, a thirty-year-old man and a teenager—today's society would hang him," she laughed. "How completely ludicrous. Henry and I built a wonderful life together. He actually allowed me to attend college, and our marriage lasted fifty-three years!"

"He raped you?" I asked in a hushed voice.

"Of course not! He only pushed me a little because I was young and oblivious. He nudged me when I needed it our first year. I was an immature girl who tried to resist the natural courses of marriage. I didn't know any better, but we were married, and that's part of the deal in marriage. Psst!"

She waved her hand at my startled expression.

"Just what did I expect? I cried for days after our wedding night, feeling sorry for myself. So silly, but once I straightened myself out, I slowly gained the upper hand." She stared at me proudly. "Especially after the boys came. Be an ironclad mother, and the father has no choice but to bend to your will. He'll lose everything if he steps out of line, everything. You'll see. He'll jump when you say jump, go when you say go, live, die, whatever you determine is the best."

Poor, poor Maxine. My body trembled after that reveal. As a teenager, she had been raped by a thirty-year-old man, then stayed with him for fifty-three years and believed that was perfectly normal. No wonder the world was messed up. I didn't know what to do, so I hugged her. She brushed me off with another tsking. Did she actually believe any of her bullshit? She insisted we complete stage two of our exercises in silence.

After several rounds of quiet planks of different types, we both relaxed, drenched in sweat.

"I can see you're thinking I'm a victim, that I am brainwashed. I can feel your judgment from here," Maxine said. "But I am not a victim, and neither are the students Steve has dallied with. They probably—"

A loud noise cut her off and drew our attention down to the boat dock. We stood to have a better look. Maxine owned a flat bottom party boat and a small aluminum fishing skiff that were moored to her personal floating dock. A long, sectioned, metal walkway led to the water. It was steep when the river was low, and level when the river was high. It was currently very steep. Suddenly, a hand had moved behind the white seats of the party boat, and the entire boat rocked against the buoys more than it should.

"Someone is down there," I said.

"Stay right here, and don't let him get away," Maxine told me. "I'm going to get one of the boys. These homeless people. It isn't the first time they've slept on my boat."

As Maxine hurried toward the house, I was relieved to see Bruno moving down my drive, returning from his run. Maxine waved a hand at him and pointed toward me. He nodded and jogged in my direction.

His entire torso glistened in the morning light, and he had taken his shirt off and tucked it into the back of his tiny orange shorts. He jogged right up with big bright eyes, looking exactly like a Greek God, total muscle with six-pack abs and a smooth brown chest. My face began to reheat. How annoying! I turned to study the dock and caught sight of that hand.

"Someone is down there, in the boat," I told Bruno.

"Someone is hiding?" he said. "I'll go."

He moved quickly to the metal walkway.

"Wait," I called.

But Bruno did not wait.

He double-timed it down the metal gangplank, broad shoulders flexing as he moved. The clanking of the metal dock echoed off the river bank, and his movements got the entire structure to wobble. My pulse raced as he moved closer to the boats. Anyone could be down there, and he was not afraid. He was brave. He didn't hesitate as he stepped onto the party boat. He reached down and pulled up what looked like a brown sack of potatoes, but as the limbs began moving, it clearly became a man. They struggled a bit, but Bruno let him go. Their conversation was garbled. The man shouted distinctly,

"She did it. The devil from the house pushed him over the edge, and now he's going to get me."

They stumbled out of the boat, and Bruno directed the man toward the steep ramp. The man resisted, not wanting to go up the ramp, but Bruno pushed him forward and followed close behind. Watching his arms flex, and the way he man-handled the mystery man, was exciting. I had to admit it to myself, he was hot! Bruno easily maneuvered the man in any direction he wanted.

"I told you!" he yelled. "That devil did it! She did it!"

Bruno pushed him up the ramp, and the man's bulging eyes shot frantically around. He appeared dirty, with wild, curly hair and an unkept beard. When they got halfway up the gangway, at the bend, the man turned suddenly and flung out a long leg. His foot hit Bruno in the head, and Bruno slipped on the slick metal of the steep walkway. Bruno's shoes fought for traction as he tried to get his footing, but he fell. He hit the aluminum with a terrible racket and dropped into the river. His head bobbed up once before the flowing water pushed him into the dock.

"Bruno!"

The crazy man rushed right to the top of the gangplank. He pushed me aside, sending me to the ground hard on my ass, then he ran off, toward Chucky's house, muttering something about someone wanting to get him. I scrambled to my feet and rushed down the unsteady aluminum path to the dock.

Bruno was in the water, and the river was flowing fast. Did he know how to swim? Did he get hurt went he fell in? If I spotted him in the water, what would I do? I had no idea if that small fishing boat had any gas in the tank, and even if it did, I had no idea how to start the engine. The whole dock tilted with the waves, and I had to pause to get my balance. My pulse was racing out of control.

His head popped up on the far side of the landing. Bruno pulled himself out of the water effortlessly. He twisted to sit on the metal but saw me and quickly stood instead.

"Thank God, you're okay!" I exclaimed, halting two feet from him. My first impulse was to hug him, but we barely knew each other.

He grinned at me, looking refreshed.

"The water is cold," he said.

Indeed, it was. His skin was riddled with goosebumps, looking very awake, and the water wasn't just cold, it was dripping down him seductively, forming small rivers in the lines defining his chest, stomach, and arms. His small orange shorts were now plastered to the last hidden parts of him, snuggly, and he smiled through my scrutiny. *Gad!* Did I just lick my lips?

"You got a little cut on your…" *incredibly smooth and solid rock of a muscle…* "shoulder," I muttered, then turned back to the metal gangplank.

"It's not so bad."

He followed close behind and caught me once at the midway point, where the walkway bent and suddenly got very steep. His large, warm hand had caught my ass just in time. He gave it a helping push up, igniting a whole stream of interesting sensations.

How could this man I barely know have such a red-hot effect on me? My breath came unevenly, and it could not be from the short steep climb up the gangplank. *He's at least ten years younger*, I chastised myself, *and he is your fiancé's cousin… ex-fiancé*, I self-corrected.

"I hate this plank when the water is low," I said.

I heard him chuckle, and the sound made me instantly giddy. I could feel him directly behind me.

I slipped again at the top, and Bruno very deftly caught me. Both his hands had found my hips, then slipped up to steady me right below my armpits. His fingers brushed the sides of my breasts accidently. Good lord, I was on fire. Then, his hand skirted my ass again, picking at my shorts, making me feel completely limp.

"You have a thorn here or something. I'll get it." He cleaned off my shorts with a brushing hand.

And what perfect timing too. Steve and James both rapidly approached. The look on Steve's face was frightening. Was that jealousy? I'd never seen him jealous before.

"Hey!" Steve yelled. He started moving faster.

Bruno let go of me as we regained our balance. He took a step away, but he wasn't backing off. He moved to meet Steve and James.

"What the hell is going on?" Steve huffed. He only glanced at me but glared at Bruno. "Maxine is upset. Were you down in the boat?" he demanded. He took in Bruno's wet shorts with an incredulous scowl.

Bruno chuckled, obviously confused by the angry greeting.

"Where the hell is your shirt?" Steve demanded. He shot a raised eyebrow my way.

"There was a man in the party boat, and he pushed Bruno into the river," I said quickly. "He ran off that way." I flung my hand toward Chucky's house.

James finally caught up. He looked Bruno up and down, confused, then turned toward Chucky's house. He pointed that way and started moving.

"Maybe we can catch him." James ran off.

Bruno moved to follow, but Steve grabbed his arm. The two men were exactly the same height, but their mass was distributed differently.

My systems were going out of whack watching them square off. *Is this aggression over me?*

Bruno pulled his arm back and met Steve's hostility with a steady eye. They stared each other down for a few moments while I held my breath. The absurdity suddenly got me.

"Oh, stop this nonsense," I scolded Steve. "He only caught me when I slipped. His shirt fell off in the water, and that man pushed his way up here and ran off."

"What did he want?"

"He didn't stop to chat," I snapped. "He ran off."

"He didn't say anything?"

I shook my head. "Nothing that made sense."

Bruno nodded. "He did not seem well."

James jogged back from Chucky's house, and we all stopped talking to watch him close in. He shook his head when he reached us, and he paused to catch his breath. He glanced down the embankment to the river and boats.

"Nobody was back there," he said. "Maybe if we drive toward Swabbies, we'll bump into him. There's a small tent encampment under the freeway. Maybe he'll end up there. Do you think he left anything on the boat?" James pointed to the low dock. "Maybe he'll come back. I'm going to go down and take a look. Did he say anything to anyone?"

"He fears that maybe someone, perhaps a woman, is after him," Bruno said.

That made Steve suddenly laugh.

"No kidding. He's upset over a woman? Aren't we all?"

Bruno smiled. "He said that a man from the house does not like him on the boat. He also said that a beautiful devil pushed someone over the edge of the cliff and cursed all men with death. He believes the devil cursed him, and he fears for his life."

Our small circle suddenly got quiet.

"Does he mean the devil is a woman or a man?" James looked at the mansion. "Did he mean this house?"

Steve stared at me.

"He is not well," Bruno said. "Perhaps he thinks of his own house. The one he is running from. He said his wife has another man, and they threw him out, into the world. He is not well."

"None of that makes any sense at all," James said.

Chapter 6

The police arrived as we gathered in the large kitchen for brunch. Maxine invited Officer Bane and his partner Pete Webber for coffee and food, and the two officers accepted the coffee happily. They hoped to speak to each of us individually to clear up a few minor items regarding Alex's accident.

Bruno had yet to change out of his small orange shorts because Maxine insisted he first drink a cup of coffee and eat something right away. He sat on the back patio wrapped in a large beach towel. He had taken his soaking tennis shoes off and laid them out on the deck to dry. Officer Webber went out back to ask him a few questions.

"You're not here about the homeless guy on the boat?" Steve asked.

Officer Bane shook his head. He looked at Maxine.

"Is there a complaint you'd like to file? Another vagrant?"

"Oh, no, no. It doesn't do any good, does it?" Maxine waved her hand. "From time to time, they try sleeping on the pontoon, but no one ever finds them when I report them."

"I'll be happy to write it up," Shane said. "Can you tell me any specifics?"

"Brown rain jacket, dirty jeans, curly wild hair and beard, mostly grey with a little brown, about as tall as Steve, and thin. Very thin," I said.

Officer Bane wrote it all down. I glanced at Steve and caught him with the same weird expression he had flashed at me outside. Officer Bane asked Steve to step into the next room to privately chat. James and Aster lounged at the table, staring into their coffee mugs. James whispered something to her, and she shifted around to ignore him. He said something else, and that made her scoff at him.

"Grandma Maxine," Aster stood up from the table. "Call up Daxter because I wasn't kidding about me and Chucky." She shot me a nice wide-eyed smile. "My betrothed resupplied my mint tin if you're interested," she chuckled. "I've got plenty of choices, so you can be picky."

James shot her a murderous look. His entire face had turned crimson.

"You are not funny, Aster. You need to take it easy with your joking around," James warned.

She paused and smiled prettily. "I'm not joking, and I'm not letting you two assholes win."

She gave me a long stare down before pushing into the next room to interrupt Steve and the policeman.

James had risen with clenched hands. His eyes went to Maxine, and his expression changed from anger to concern. He rushed around the kitchen island and grabbed her at the waist. She slumped into his arms.

"Maxine!" I went to her other side to help steady her.

"Let's check her sugar level." He quickly left.

"Oh, poor Aster. She's hurting and grasping at straws. It's going to give me a heart attack. These kids refusing to get along," Maxine wheezed.

James returned quickly and proceeded to prick Maxine in the finger. Barely any blood came out, and he had to squeeze her finger. I stared at his pensive face.

"It's okay, that's plenty for the test," he said.

We managed to get Maxine into a chair, and James finished the readout.

"Well, it's not your sugar."

"That's good because I broke my fancy poker pen this morning." Maxine let out a little chuckle.

"You can have mine, I haven't used it yet." James gave her a small smile. "I've got a vial and needles as backup. I actually prefer doing it the old-fashioned way. But what are we going to do about this fainting spell? Shall we give your doctor a call? Maxine, where is your nurse today? What time does she come? Shouldn't she be here by now?"

"I gave Kira the week off," Maxine told him. "With everyone here, I didn't think she'd be needed. Perhaps we better give Doctor Hoover a call."

James nodded, and Maxine pointed to where her phone lay on the counter. I fetched it.

Steve and Officer Bane came back into the room. I spied Aster outside talking to the other officer and Bruno. Both those fellows did not appear comfortable with whatever Aster had to say. Steve came round and tapped me on the shoulder. We exchanged places, and just before I followed Officer Bane into the next room, Steve winked at me.

"I got you covered," he mouthed.

What in the world does that mean?

In the next room, Officer Bane watched the interaction on the back patio with his hands on his hips.

"We're just touching base, to see if anybody remembers anything new." He noticed me. "Apparently, the crime scene team doesn't believe the fall was an accident, at least not yet. There appear to be suspicious muddy prints along the levy, so we're double checking if anyone heard or saw anything. The added mention of a vagrant is concerning, but they're usually pretty harmless. Do you have anything new to add?"

"I've got nothing new," I told him.

He nodded, turning his attention back to the three people on the porch.

"Aster is odd," he said. "Has she shown any signs of grieving? Maybe it hasn't quite sunk in about her brother. Have you noticed anything strange about her?"

"People grieve in odd ways," I offered.

He may not know about the pills, and I wasn't going to tell him. Anyone could see that Aster was drowning her feelings in a well of drugs, and she did not trust her cousins, or Maxine, with her feelings. She was lost.

"Did you know that Alex Winters called 911 the other night?"

That surprised me, and I shook my head.

"He used a temporary phone, so we didn't put it together right away. But he called some time before midnight and stated that Steve was trying to kill him.

That's the main reason we've been asked to requestion everyone."

The tension drained out of me.

"Oh, yes." I nodded. "Those two got into a silly fight, right out there on the patio, a scuffle. I'm surprised he actually called 911. He threatened to, but I thought he was just talking. Alex had been pretty drunk that night."

Officer Bane nodded. "Steve Winters claims that the man from the boat said that Aster pushed her brother down the levy. Did you hear the boatman say anything like that? It's suspicious because Aster claims she was with Chuck Collins, your next-door neighbor, pretty much until dawn, so it doesn't add up."

I shook my head. "The homeless guy never mentioned Aster. He made some ranting comments about a devil. And he said that the devil pushed a man over the levy."

"Are you certain? Mr. Winters was pretty adamant that the man named Aster."

"I'm not sure why Steve would tell you that. He must have jumped to that conclusion. Only Bruno and I actually heard the homeless man anyway, and he didn't mention any names. He was afraid of the *devil from the house*, but he didn't specify which house."

I pressed my lips together. No one could blame Steve for jumping to conclusions. When that man said the *devil from the house*, my mind instantly jumped to the same conclusion, Aster. She was slightly scary in several different ways.

"Chuck Collins will probably corroborate her statement, but he is not exactly a reliable witness."

Officer Bane stared out the window at Aster. His hands rested on his hip belt with a finger tapping the handcuffs.

Was he considering arresting her based on Steve's conclusions? Did he find her suspicious? She certainly seemed odd to me, but could Aster have pushed her own twin over the levy? Maybe. But one thing is certain, she told the truth about being at Chucky's house. She didn't lie about that, and there was another witness that could place her there: me.

"She was there," I said softly. "At Chucky's. I saw her there. It was late, and I don't recall the exact time, but I imagine she had been there for quite some time before I saw her and planned to stay a bit longer."

Now I had Officer Bane's full attention.

"Sometimes I take a late-night walk if I can't sleep. That night, I happened to go in that direction. I saw both Chucky and Aster in his backyard, by the firepit... occupied."

"Steve Winters claims that both of you were in your bungalow, together, the entire night. Just a minute ago, he made it clear that you two were together all night. Did he go on the walk with you?"

"No," I shook my head. "I went alone, he was asleep on the couch."

"Was he still asleep when you returned? Maybe he slept through your walk."

But he hadn't been sleeping when I got back. In fact, Steve hadn't been in the bungalow at all. He had been missing for the rest of the night, until the next morning when Adam and the dog found Alex in the beaver's dam.

Why in the world would he lie to the police? The hair on the back of my neck bristled. Did he use me as an alibi? Why would he need an alibi?

My eyes went toward the door to the other room, where Steve waited with the others. Steve, the fiancé with whom I had shared intimate moments. Who was he? Could he have killed his own cousin?

I blinked back those thoughts. No! Whatever happened, it must have been an accident. When I glanced back at Officer Bane, it was quite clear that he knew exactly what I was thinking, *Steve could not be trusted.*

Steve was angry.

The two police officers asked him to go to the station to make an official statement, and he gave me a long, narrow-eyed stare. He wasn't required to go to the station, but if he didn't, someone else would be back with a more official request.

My skin prickled wondering why he threw Aster under the bus on that crazy man's ranting. My mind replayed how Alex had jumped so quickly in accusation during the fight. He insisted Steve tried to kill him and even felt strongly enough to call the police. At first, it all seemed like a heated, drunken episode, but was it? Did Steve push Alex over the levy wall? Did he have a violent side carefully hidden away? Was it finally coming to light?

I studied my former fiancé, wondering if I had ever known him at all. A few weeks ago, he had been a sweet, charming, doting lover, but now some of his hidden secrets had emerged. Coercing young students to feed a dark deviant side I never expected, a thirst for his sizable trust fund, cold heartless interactions with his cousins, and violence. He showed no hesitation in punching his cousin in the neck. And though Aster wasn't mourning in a normal way, Steve hadn't been upset, either. When they hauled up that body, he hadn't even blinked.

He nodded in agreement with Officer Bane and left in his own car.

Aster snorted and disappeared into her room to sleep.

Maxine gathered items for a trip to the doctor. She insisted on opening every pill bottle to check the contents and ended up spilling little white pills everywhere. Bruno, James, and I dropped to the floor to gather them up. Maxine was moving around much better, but still a little slow. She threw the near-empty medical containers into her large purse and told us to throw the spilled pills into a baggie. Her old eyes were weary as she smiled weakly at me.

"I'm going to check on Aster before we leave," she whispered softly. "That poor girl is lashing out at everyone. No, you stay here. I'll manage myself now, and she might be more comfortable if it's just me popping in. Don't you worry about me now. I'm a tough old gal."

We watched as she slowly drifted down the hall to her granddaughter's room. Poor Maxine.

Bruno quickly excused himself to get cleaned up.

James shuffled through Maxine's medicine, rearranging them. He seemed unsure of what to do with the bagged pills we picked up.

"Maybe I'll put them in the sharp objects disposal."

He also hurried out of the room, leaving me confused and alone.

Chapter 7

The Sacramento River dribbled along quietly on summer nights, but it roared quite noisily during the day. Boats and jet skis raced by with motor noises that echoed off the tall walls of the river banks, often followed by high-pitched voices mixed with laughter. On the Garden Highway side, motorcycles zoomed around the bend, coming or going to riverside bars upstream or to Old Town Sacramento downstream.

I lounged sunning on my elevated deck patio with a notebook and pen, taking in the water activity on the river. I felt his footsteps before he poked his head around the corner—not who I expected.

"Hello," Bruno said hesitantly.

He was fully dressed, clean-shaven, and fresh from a shower. His hair was dark, almost jet black, as were the long eyelashes circling his bright eyes. All his coloring was just slightly darker than Steve's, so they weren't so identical after the first glance.

He carried something behind his back, a bottle of wine, and in the other hand, two glasses and an opener. He smiled down at me in my bikini. I sat up straighter and set my notebook down, feeling my face heat, glancing around. No coverup handy, and why would there be while sunning on my own back patio outlining a section of Maxine's memoir?

"I hope I am not troubling you," he said. "But no one is here, except Aster, and she has gone to sleep."

"Oh, no bother," I said softly. Poor Bruno, abandoned by the family he did not know.

He presented the bottle of wine.

"Would you care to sample some wine? It's from my home."

I nodded quickly, feeling ridiculous for my earlier embarrassment. He grinned and sat across from me. He got busy opening the bottle.

"When you say it's from your home, do you mean that your family makes wine?"

He flashed a large and proud smile, handsome. It was infectious. He popped the cork and waved the open bottle top around.

"We have a small winery hugging the hills near Bento Goncalves," he gushed. "Perhaps you did not know, but my father studied wine at the university here, near Sacramento. He has a degree in viticulture and enology from the university in Davis. His dream was always to make wine, and that is why he traveled to Brazil."

"Wow, I had no idea."

Bruno poured a nice sample of clear white into large glasses and offered one to me. I copied how he swirled it in his glass before taking a sip. It was pleasant, not too sweet, not too dry, and a bit fruity. I didn't really know anything about fine wines, but his was quite nice. He set the bottle on the table, and the label caught my eye. A light blue teardrop-shaped crystal was drawn under the name, *Paraiba Tears*.

"It's good," I told him.

"Thank you." He grinned. "I brought six bottles and hoped to share it sooner, but the correct time has not presented itself. It is from the first cask we made together as father and son when I was only sixteen, ten years ago. I thought I would bring it here to his family, and I would make a toast to him, for meeting his dreams. To let them know he was fulfilled."

Bruno blinked. His long lashes fluttered rapidly for a moment. He shrugged and gave me a simple smile. I held my glass up.

"To your father," I said. "For realizing his dreams."

He nodded, "Thank you."

We both took a sip of the sweet wine. He lounged back in his chair and turned his eyes to the river. Sitting with Bruno was relaxing. Unlike Steve, he did not need to fill up the quiet with a steady stream of words about sports and cars. He lounged back and closed his eyes, enjoying the warm sun. *Twenty-six years old!* Seven years my junior, and here I was stealing glimpses at him. It was wrong, wrong, wrong, for more than one reason.

A flutter passed overhead, and Bruno sat up, searching the sky. He turned to me and pointed at the devil's oak tree.

I chuckled, nodding. "Have you seen him?"

"Her," he smiled. "*She* is too large to be male."

"Are you positive? I'm convinced that owl is male."

He shook his head. "And her voice is too sweet," he smiled at me. "She is certainly female. Beautiful, wise, dangerous."

His piercing eyes were too much to take, and I glanced away. He poured more wine into our glasses, and I didn't protest. Energy emanated from Bruno, and all I could think about was those hard pecs and abs under his shirt, his smooth skin. He shifted, and those wet, orange, clinging shorts popped into my head. *He's seven years younger*, I told myself, *and your ex-fiancé's cousin!* Not to mention, he was in mourning.

"She is a young mother, no doubt," he smiled.

"A mother? How can you tell?"

"She's cautious, and it's the right time for her, three months after winter." He shrugged. "Of course, I'm no expert."

I glanced back at that oak tree. Could she have a *baby* in there?

He asked about my family back east, the grandmother who raised me, my dead parents. He inquired about my likes, my favorite color, ice cream flavor, book, movie, song, food, and anything to make small talk. He wanted to know why I practiced yoga and if I did other sports, and he laughed with delight at almost everything I said. He claimed to love my voice, sweet like the owl, and I realized that Bruno was flirting with me. That young cousin had just as much charm as his older look-a-like. For a brief moment, I was angry at him.

Then, he turned serious and stared at the large mansion beside us.

"Is it only this family? Is this normal for Americans, how they are behaving?"

His eyes were wounded. He was disappointed with his American relatives.

"No, not normal," I told him. "But these are unusual circumstances and…"

His penetrating eyes bore into mine, searching for answers I didn't have.

"I only just met James and Aster and… and Alex," I told him. "The same day I met you, the night he… We're probably witnessing people in shock, surrounded by a family they barely know. Truthfully, Maxine never said much about any of them, and Steve never talked about them either, except maybe James, in passing. I'm as surprised as you at… at everything."

He nodded and emptied the wine into our large glasses. "My father. He told me all about this family. He was an open and honest man. He wanted to wash his hands of them. We could not understand his heart, my mother and me. My mother always wanted him to make amends, and I agreed with her. How could he forget his family so completely? But now, I think I am beginning to understand a little of his feelings. My only regret is that I came too late to meet my only brother. If I'd gotten here half a day earlier, I could have met him. My chance is lost forever."

"What about James? He's your brother too."

The expression on Bruno's face! He blinked rapidly, confused. "The life history, you are writing it for Maxine. Does it not include many unfortunate events?" he asked.

"Well, yes."

"But she did not tell you of her children or grandchildren?"

"Well, no," I said. "I'm ghostwriting her early years. Up until she marries. Someone else helped her with the later years, the children, and the death of her husband. Truthfully, the early years had already been written, but she wanted a rewrite of them. Maxine and I grew up in the same city and went to the same schools, elementary, high school, and even college. She thought the original pages lacked authenticity, were glossed over."

"Amazing," he said. "So, you are unaware of the history of my father at all?"

"Well, she has hinted at a few things, but for the most part, no. She did say he was disinherited for several reasons."

"I'll tell you everything," he sat up. "James is not my brother. He is actually my cousin. My father's first wife *knew* his own brother, my uncle, Steve's father. You know what I mean?"

He waited, and I nodded, but I was still processing that.

"They were lovers, and my uncle tricked my father, his young brother, into marrying his mistress because he was already a married man. That is what my father told me. The mistress, James's mother, seduced him and claimed he impregnated her, so he married her because he believed she loved him and he was smitten with her. But my father discovered the truth after James was born, because his brother still carried on the affair, even after she was his brother's wife… and my father, he was heartbroken. He said he had been young and stupid, and his own parents refused to listen to him. They did not wish to own such a scandalous story."

My mouth was hanging open.

"My father could not accept his situation and left. In his broken-hearted grief, he behaved badly for a short time, and the twins were conceived. He did not know their mother well, but he knew they were not compatible. Their relationship, it was one of business, her business. It was not his finest moment, but he did ensure his allowance was provided for them. He made a deal with his own father regarding that allowance. It was his trade-off for not causing trouble or shining a light on matters regarding his wife and brother."

Bruno appeared slightly embarrassed about that information.

"That is when he moved to Brazil, to begin again. He found a hill of barren land and built a winery. He met my mother in Paraiba, and it was love at first sight. My father told me, *when you see the woman meant for you, you know it the moment you look into her eyes.*"

Bruno's eyes bore into mine, and my entire body felt it. I could barely swallow. He smiled shyly at me, then reached for the empty bottle of wine.

"They worked hard together, building a home and working the land. In the beginning, they could not marry, because his wife would not divorce him. Many tears of grief were shed. But, after his first wife died, my parents could finally marry. Then, there were tears of joy."

"Paraiba tears?"

He nodded. "Yes, Paraiba tears, both happy and sad."

"Does James know?"

Bruno shook his head. "I'm not sure, but it appears, no."

"What about the cancer? James thinks he left because of the cancer."

Bruno shook his head again. "I don't know anything about cancer."

"Maxine said James lost his mother to cancer."

"My father never said anything about cancer," Bruno said. "I only know that his first wife died in a car accident, along with his brother, my uncle. They died together. It allowed my parents to finally marry. Then, I was born."

Did Maxine get it wrong? She said Steve's father died in that accident with his own wife. Was it Steve's mother who had cancer? Maxine was practically ninety years old, so maybe she was losing parts of her memory and mixed them up, her daughters-in-law. She always seemed sharp as a tack, but who knew if that was just the façade of her strong personality. Or maybe she wanted to remember it wrong.

"My parents shared many happy years together," Bruno said.

"Oh, Bruno." I reached out to cover his hand.

The slight electric shock surprised me, and I almost pulled my hand back, but I kept it over his and pressed my lips together. He shared deeply personal secrets with me, and I could not let my own physical frustrations keep me from offering him a little human kindness.

He smiled and placed a hot, large hand over mine. His hand was gigantic and looked extremely strong. God, why did that flood my chest with liquid warmth? His left eyebrow went up to alter his face into irresistible cuteness. It was uncanny to watch a face with such familiar characteristics look so fresh and new. Steve was certainly handsome, but he was nowhere near as adorable as Bruno.

"Now it's your turn," he said softly.

"My turn?"

"To speak about something hard, such as, why you are involved with my cousin. He does not seem right for you."

I took my hand away.

"I'm sorry," he said.

His cute smile faded, and he shrank into himself, looking ashamed. I shook my head quickly.

"It's okay," I told him. "But I feel the need to tell you, Steve and I were recently engaged. I wasn't just dating your cousin, we had plans to marry. Right now, we're going through a rough spot, and I am not certain how it's going to turn out."

Bruno swung his legs around and faced me head-on. His expression turned serious and his undivided attention produced a nervous chuckle from me.

"When two people are as serious as thinking about marriage, it's hard to turn everything off. I fell in love with Steve, I think, and it's hard not to trust what he tells me."

"But your instincts tell you not to trust him?"

"I got my feelings hurt," I corrected him. "I guess, I romanticized him a little too much. Maybe it isn't his fault that he's just a normal man."

"You deserve romantic." Bruno's eyes slid down to my neck. That made me hold my breath for a second. I shook it off.

"He is romantic. He is very romantic. Believe me, your cousin is an extremely romantic man. He was hard to resist."

Every bit of that was true. Steve enjoyed showering me with attention, I was spoiled. Not a week passed without a fancy dinner date, flowers, a sweet text message, small notes on my pillow, or a plethora of blandishments.

"I believe he is too old for you," Bruno said. "He is, maybe, forty years old?"

"He's forty-one," I smirked. "Not too old. I'm not as young as you might imagine."

His eyes passed over me with an odd expression. Was he trying to age me? His quick survey lit my nerves on fire and made me realize I should find something to throw over my swimsuit. I stood up and moved to the sliding door of my patio, getting my libido back under control.

"Would you like some ice water?" I asked. "I think the wine has gone to my head. I may need to take a nap."

"Yes, please. Water is nice." He hesitated but followed me into the bungalow. "I believe he is too old for you, but I can see how you find him romantic."

"Yes, yes, he's very romantic," I told Bruno. "He even designed my engagement ring. He found a stone that matched my eyes, had it circled with diamonds, and commissioned a jeweler to make a one-of-a-kind engagement ring. *That is undeniably romantic.* I absolutely love that ring. It may be a coincidence, but the mineral on your wine bottle is a similar color."

I filled two glasses with water and passed one to him.

Bruno glanced around the bungalow, taking in my desk and laptop in the corner, the bookshelf, and finally, the half wall to my messy bedroom. I felt myself flush when his eyes paused on my unmade bed. He turned back and locked his eyes on mine. It was hard to look at him while breathing in a normal way. He seemed to fill the entire room with his presence, and my imagination kept playing out erotic what-ifs. What if he took off that shirt? What if he grabbed me and kissed me, and we ended up on the messy bed? Would I resist? Then, the image of his wet orange shorts invaded my mind, and my entire private area flamed with desire.

"Do you want to see the ring?" I asked softly, turning away.

Bruno did.

I walked directly to my desk and pulled out the drawer. My heart was pounding in my ears. What would he do if I jumped on him? What would he do if I stopped and gently kissed his neck? What would he do if I grabbed his ass?

My fingers closed around the beautiful engagement ring Steve had designed. *Blue of your eyes, diamonds to last forever*, he had said. Damn, I had consumed too much wine on an empty stomach. My mind should not be thinking what-ifs about a man seven years younger than me. That was too large of an age gape! I need to get back on track with my thoughts.

"This design came from a dream, immediately after we met, he claimed." My voice came out in a whisper. "He dreamed of us… and this ring appeared in his dream, he said. He woke and knew we were meant to be together."

I gulped guiltily as I admired the glittering jewels, a promise of our life together. My blood raced in my chest because I loved that ring, but I wasn't sure if I still loved the man who gave it to me. It was a sign, wasn't it? Steve designing a ring I absolutely adored. I didn't slip it back on my finger, instead I presented it in the palm of my hand, and Bruno stared down at it with his lips pressed together. He nodded.

"It is a beautiful ring," he said weakly. "Truly, and it suits you perfectly."

"I love this ring, I really do." I dropped it back into the drawer and shut it. "So, you see, very romantic. Tell me of any other girl whose fiancé designed a one-of-a-kind engagement ring so perfectly. Our grandkids will love that story."

Bruno had suddenly moved close to me, he stood inches away. My blood pulsed as my eyes stared at his collar bone, neck, shoulders, and the bottom of his ears hanging just below his hairline. My nose became flooded with his scent. He licked his lower pink lip, and I wobbled. I had definitely overindulged because I felt slightly dizzy.

"Don't have grandkids with him," Bruno whispered. "You shouldn't trust what he tells you. Trust your instincts. Your instincts are good."

My eyes became hypnotized by his lips, and my hands had a mind of their own. They slid up his solid and muscular chest, where they had been itching to be all morning. Then, my hands migrated to his arms. His biceps were quite an upgrade, and though I meant to push him away, my hands ran up to caress his shoulders instead. He didn't move an inch but gazed down at me, and his perusal felt erotic.

What am I doing?

His pink lips were descending toward me, and every brain cell in my head screamed, *YES!* I ran my hands behind his solid, chorded neck and pulled him closer. His lips sent pulses down my torso, flooding me with silky warm pleasure, and my entire body melted into his. He kissed me deep, then deeper, infusing me in passion, and I felt him everywhere. No one had ever kissed me like that. His lips brushed mine softly before his mouth went to my neck to nibble a path to my ear. *My goodness, Bruno!* His large hands were everywhere, and anywhere they touched, a small trail of fire remained.

"When I first saw you," he whispered in my ear, "I felt something for you. I felt that this must happen."

He held me in a soft embrace.

"I enjoy being around you," he said. "I feel safe."

"It's nice being around you too." I swallowed.

He pulled slightly away and stared into my eyes. Then, he pulled his shirt over his head and tossed it onto my desk making me gasp again. His torso was a perfectly carved, hard and smooth, body of a Greek God in all its prime glory. Did it matter that Bruno was practically a stranger to me? Or that he was the cousin of the man I was supposed to love, or that we would only know each other for a few more days?

"You are beautiful." His breath came heavy.

What was I doing? Things had escalated too fast and felt out of control. I felt like an immature girl, and Bruno was seven years my junior. But wasn't Steve eight years my senior? I'd never once thought that was wrong. A realization hit me. Bruno and I were closer in age than Steve and me.

"We can't get carried away," I said. "I'm just recently out of a relationship."

"No, I promise," he said. "We won't get carried away. I understand. You are sleepy and have consumed much wine, and we are not long friends yet. But I feel able to finally breathe here, with you, and you are the only one I trust here. I'm also tired. Can we lay down together, just to rest?"

"I can't…"

"I promise," he said. "This will not go any further than what you want, but the need to hold you, I feel it strongly. Can we stay close together while we rest? I will be grateful. I feel out of place in that house. I feel alone, anxious, and being near you makes me happy. I can relax over here."

His eyes were uneasy, and maybe even… fearful? Perhaps he felt we were both outsiders and could take refuge from that clan of cold relatives together. He needed someone to comfort him. That was what his eyes said, and even though we'd barely met, he trusted me to do it.

"Okay, but this cannot go any further."

"I promise," he nodded. "We will do nothing but sleep."

"Maybe not nothing," I said softly. "Maybe we can kiss one or two more times."

He nodded. "Yes, I agree."

In the next moment, Bruno pulled me against him, crushing us together, ravaging my lips with his in a sensual kiss. He didn't just keep me from falling, he swept me up into his arms effortlessly.

"Can I carry you?" he asked. "Since when you lost your shoe, I've been dreaming of carrying you somewhere. You look nice to carry."

That made me laugh, and he laughed with me. Then, he carried me around the short half-wall to gently place me on my unkept bed, where the kissing continued.

Chapter 8

The ringing woke me up. My cell phone, next to the bed, rang and rang. It was set to ring twice before going to voice mail, but whoever was calling tried more than once. The glowing display made a groan escape my lips, *Steve*.

I turned to the large, half-naked, male in my bed, Bruno, and felt guilty, guilty, guilty for the incredibly erotic kissing session we shared. My life had fast become a tangled mess, and it did not escape me that my behavior would be hurtful to someone. That someone who was on the phone.

Bruno roused and rolled over. The sight of him made my face heat with pleasure. It wasn't just his young fit body that attracted me, there was something adorable radiating from him too, something that made me feel completely comfortable in my own skin. The way he gazed at me, how he listened to me, how in sync those kisses were, the cuddling, and he had kept his promise. All we had done was kiss and cuddle and nap, though he easily could have enticed me into more. I felt something enormous for him in my chest. What was it?

Had it started the other night when our eyes had met for the first time? Had the jolt I felt been love at first sight? Was that possible?

Bruno opened his pretty eyes and gathered me into his warm arms to cradle. I slid right in without hesitation. Staying right there, forever, sounded pretty nice.

But the message on my phone was not going to go away.

"Bruno?"

He nuzzled his nose into my neck.

"Bruno."

"Please allow me to breath your scent a little longer." He inhaled deeply. "You smell like heaven."

"Bruno, that was Steve on the phone. He left the police station and is coming here."

He moved away but didn't let me go.

"Seeing you here is going to hurt him," I said. "And I don't want to hurt him like this."

He loosened his hold on me with a worried expression.

"I will tell him eventually," I said. "Just not like this."

"It is over with you and him?"

"Yes," I said.

"And maybe it's beginning with you and me?"

I nodded my head slowly. "Maybe."

He beamed, and his entire body embraced mine. I could stay there forever, rolling in his exquisite aura. But then, we felt the vibrations of someone walking down the plank walkway. The footfalls were familiar. We tensed in alarm.

Bruno jumped out of bed and searched for his shirt, hunting for any evidence. I looked for a cover-up and quickly pulled on a stray t-shirt, one Steve had left for me. I frantically pointed for Bruno to go into the other room. At any minute, Steve would be at the back door and have a clear view of my bedroom.

"My shirt?"

"You threw it on the desk." My voice sounded frantic. "Go out the other door. But don't go down the stairs, they shake the whole house. You might have to hide by the door and wait for a little while."

Bruno nodded and rushed into the main room. He knocked something over before rushing to the far door. He paused to blow me a kiss just as a rapid knocking commenced on my back bedroom door. My head swung around, and I spotted Steve's face in the small square window staring right at me. His eyes lit up at seeing me, and I realized I was plastered in a gigantic grin. I wiped it off my face as he opened the door and walked right in like he had done a hundred times before.

"Hey!" I pulled the sheet up to cover my bare legs.

His eyes trailed over me in his seductive way, pausing on my shirt. That stupid t-shirt! He loved when I wore his shirts. He took the two steps to the bed and stared down at me.

"Taking an afternoon nap?" he grinned.

His eyes trailed over the sheet covering my legs and stopped on a colorful patch of material. My recently missing bikini top lay on the edge of the bed, and he let out an amused chuckle as I reached for it. I quickly hid the top under the sheet and felt my face heat up several degrees under his scrutiny. He seemed to enjoy my discomfort.

"Did I catch you using your little toy?" His voice was soft, husky.

"Gad! Your mind," I hissed.

He felt free to sit on the edge of the bed.

"I know you enjoy the afternoon. Can I watch? Or join you?"

I gave him a scathing scowl.

"Come on, Amanda, it's been over a week, and we both know we're going to make up, get married, and live a long happy life. Let's start right now."

His hand found my foot, and he squeezed it through the sheet before I moved it away.

"You were ready to forgive me last night, before Aster's little joke. We can make up right now and not waste your favorite time of day. We can put this whole silly episode behind us."

He scooted closer, and his hand found my leg under the sheet. He was licking his lips and staring at my thin tee using his puppy dog eyes. I moved away, feeling disgusted with him, with me, with the two of us.

"I'm in agony over here, and you are too. You have no idea what seeing you in those crumpled sheets does to me."

I squirmed out of the bed and went into the other room. Thankfully, there was no sign of Bruno. No sign that he had been in the house at all. It felt empty. I wondered if he was hiding on the porch.

Steve followed close behind and grabbed me into a back hug. His hands made a pass over my breasts, and he tried to kiss the sweet spot behind my ear. He held fast, even as I tried to wriggle out of his grasp. He chuckled like we were playing, and it infuriated me because we sometimes played that way, wrestling, in the past, and I always loved it. Finally, I squirmed out of his hands and put the kitchen island between us. I glared at him.

"Oh, come on, baby." His eyes stared at his old college t-shirt as if he could see through it. Maybe he could, it *was* thin. "You know you want to make-up."

"It's not going to happen. We are not getting back together," I said firmly.

He locked eyes with mine, and for a moment, he appeared menacing. My pulse raced, but unlike all the other times my pulse raced with him, this time it raced with fear. His secret closet crowded my mind, and the thumb drive with the video clips, that girl tied down. He said they were play-acting, but parts of their play did not appear consenting. Could he escalate what we had done to that? He could easily claim he thought we were *playing* because sometimes we had played a little rough. *Could Steve actually attack me, completely overpower me, and force me?*

"You've been lying to me," I said.

He snorted, and surprisingly, that calmed me down.

"I've been protecting you." He raised his eyebrows at me. "All I ever do is protect you."

"From what?"

"From this. Your judgmental attitude. I hid that box because of this, your attitude. I knew you would paint it all black, and I was protecting you. I wasn't hiding or keeping secrets, I was protecting you from seeing something that you don't understand and equating it to that story you told me. The one about your own college experience."

"You were protecting me? That's what you're calling it?"

"What do you call it?" He waved his hands around.

"Asshole, criminal behavior that sickens me when I think about it. You've crossed a line with your students, Steve. You're the worst type of man imaginable."

He frowned angrily. "Is that why you pointed the finger at me with that policeman?"

"I didn't point a finger."

His menacing face appeared again.

"I didn't know you lied to the police, Steve," I said. "Why did you do that? Why did you tell them we were together all night, implying we could vouch for each other? What are you hiding?"

His eyes bulged.

"I was protecting you again!" He pointed. "You!"

I shook my head.

"Listen, sweetheart. The police are convinced someone forcefully pushed Alex over the levy edge and then left him for dead, and I happen to have personal experience with your surprisingly violent temper. And that homeless man claimed a beautiful devil pushed Alex over the edge, all while cursing men. Does that sound familiar to you? Because it sounds familiar to me, my beautiful little spitfire."

He stared at me. I said nothing.

"Just fess up, Amanda. Did you bump into Alex on your nightly walk? Did he do something stupid? Try to grab you or try to stick his fat tongue down your throat, or did he say something lewd? I can see him doing all of those things. Did you attack him back with the same kind of anger you used on me?"

His voice calmed down, and he took my hands in his. I was still trying to process what he was saying. *Did he believe I pushed Alex over the levy wall?*

"It's okay, Amanda. I love you. No one needs to know about it, ever. He was a classic ass, an idiot, and I'm sure you didn't mean for him to take a branch through the gut when he fell. It was an unfortunate accident, and don't worry, I did not tell the police about your wicked left hook. As far as anyone knows, you couldn't hurt a fly."

"What are you talking about?" I stared at him. "Are you trying to gaslight me again? You're the one he was afraid of. You're the one who lied to the police. You're the one who wasn't on the couch where I left you and went mysteriously missing."

His entire face creased, and he took his hands back.

"I'm telling you that I will protect you from whatever you might have done." His voice boomed. "I won't let anybody point a finger at you."

Who was he trying to convince? Me? Himself? My skin prickled.

"Your bruised hand gave you away, sweetheart." He pointed to my knuckles. "How'd you get that bruise, Amanda? Not on my eye, I can tell you that. Who'd you hit?"

"What? I hit my hand on your grandmother's coffee table," I countered. "The real question is, where did you disappear to the other night?"

"I went looking for you!" He threw his hands up in exasperation.

He fidgeted in frustration, and I was no longer afraid of him. This was his normal state of anger, one that I was very familiar with. He wasn't acting, *was he?* He shook his head at me.

"I woke up, and you were gone, and I went out to look for you. I actually hiked all the way the hell down to that little beach you like, then came back just before sunrise. I was tired as hell and dirty as shit and got cleaned up in the house. I crashed in the basement playroom because I was embarrassed to be seen sleeping on the den couch. We are supposed to be engaged!"

Could that be true? It definitely sounded true.

"Well, we're not engaged, not anymore. And hitting you last week, your eye. I'm sorry about that, but it's because you've wound me up in your web of lies and debauchery, and I got anxious. I don't go around hitting people, but you made me fall in love with my worst nightmare. I cannot continue this, and I can't believe you actually thought I pushed Alex into the beaver's dam."

He stared at me, unmoving.

But there was movement outside the window. *Oh my God, Bruno!* He was sneaking across the back patio, tiptoeing comically toward the empty wine bottle and glasses. I nearly smiled at him when he glanced up. He winked.

"Look, sweetheart," Steve said. "I know you're upset, but don't make any rash decisions about us, not yet. This has been a hectic week, and we probably shouldn't lash out at each other in our current states of mind. Let's hold off saying or doing anything that might cause lasting damage to our relationship. Calling me your *worst nightmare* is pretty hurtful."

He moved to turn around, so I quickly sprang forward to keep him from facing the patio. Bruno noticed and gave me a thumbs up. *Wow, now I feel diabolical and sneaky.*

"It has been hectic," I agreed, "You're right. I'm sorry. But you actually assumed I sent Alex over that embankment and just left him there? That's a pretty low opinion of me too, pretty hurtful."

"Okay, fair. But you have been acting odd lately, and the vagrant did imply an angry woman pushed Alex." Steve flashed a Bruno-like grin. "And I know your temper, and I know Alex. He would have said or done something crass to set you off. I can easily see you knocking him off that embankment, accidentally. You are pretty strong when you're determined. I have a healthy respect for your anger."

I wrinkled my nose at him. The distance between us had closed dramatically in my attempt to keep him facing away from the patio, and I didn't want him to get the wrong idea. Bruno finally gathered up the glassware and took several gentle steps toward the walkway to the main house patio, almost out of sight. He paused to look back at me, and I almost laughed, he was too cute. I had to bite back my grin and try not to look out the window.

"Aster..." Steve said.

"What?"

"If not you, then it was Aster that did it. She must have."

He had moved just a hint closer, in an almost imperceptible move, but it put him right in my personal space, and I suddenly felt his energy touching me. I almost put my hands on his chest, to push him away, but stopped just short of touching him. Steve watched me, quizzically, confused at the mixed messages. He stared at my raised hands, and he glanced at the thin t-shirt again.

"I'm better than a toy," he barely whispered.

I waited one more second for Bruno to pass out of sight, then pushed him away and crossed my arms over my chest.

"A minute ago, you accuse me of killing your cousin, and now you want to—"

"I love you. It's a natural response. I'm sorry I accused you. Now, I can see that it must have been Aster. She's the woman the guy was talking about."

I stepped away from him.

"There is no woman, Steve. The man from the boat was deranged, not right in the head. You can't accuse poor Aster of something so horrific based on the garbled rantings of a mentally ill vagrant. Why are you so hell-bent on accusing someone of murder?"

"I don't want to accuse anyone," he said. "But the police think something was definitely suspicious about the way he fell, and that 911 call, it came much later than our scuffle on the porch. It sounded like someone was following him, and he thought it was me. He was scared out of his mind because it was so dark, and he was lost. They let me listen to the recording."

He followed me back into my bedroom, where I searched for a pair of sweat pants to add to my scanty ensemble. I was feeling overexposed in my bikini bottoms and shirt, not something I had ever felt around him before. He stood at the half wall and watched me.

"Aster is pretty sneaky, and strong… or maybe she got Chucky involved. That man is a maniac. I think he's capable of anything, and he certainly bonds with Aster, they—"

"It was an accident," I snapped. "How could you even suggest Aster would push her own brother to his death or convince Chucky to do it for her? Let's not entertain any crazy scenarios."

But deep inside, I wondered if he was onto something.

"She hated him. He was her worst bully, and she hated him. I'm surprised she didn't kill him years ago."

"You don't mean that."

"Amanda," he said. "Haven't you noticed? Those twins are freeloaders, they only came here because of some legal mumbo jumbo between my idiot uncle and grandfather. And they constantly argued over the allowance the estate allots them. It's no secret that Alex has cheated Aster out of her share with his hair-brained schemes."

There were car noises on the road. Someone blared a car horn. It often happened whenever people slowed down to dip into the upper driveway with traffic behind them. Drivers didn't like to slow down on that Garden Highway, not for residents, not for curves, and not for pedestrians. Steve backed up and put his hands in his pockets.

"It's probably Maxine and James. I'm going to find out about Maxine, then go home for a spell." He gave me a thin, defeated smile. "Sorry, babe, you missed your chance at a hot afternoon tumble. Maybe you'll get lucky later."

I locked the door behind him, a first. Locking the door between the river mansion and the guest cottage was not a common practice, but suddenly, there was someone I wanted to lock out, someone dangerous. *Who?* The more his words ran through my head, the more sense they made. Aster was not normal. She showed clear signs of hostility, with everyone, and had been ugly when she thought I had gotten back with Steve.

And she hadn't given one indication that she cared that Alex was dead.

But I had something bigger clouding my mind, a burning compulsion to fix something in my work in progress, my WIP, another bout of inspiration brewed. That male main character *could be saved* if I made a few minor adjustments. Perhaps, he could have a slight accent. Perhaps, I could make him a tad bit younger than the female main character and give him jet-black hair. Perhaps, a name change was needed, instead of *Steve*, I could change it to something cuter like… the only name that came to mind was *Bruno*.

Chapter 9

James dropped by my door a few hours later to invite me to the mansion for an after dinner cocktail. Everyone was meeting in the big den for wine from Brazil. The mention of Bruno's wine got my blood flowing, and I longed to look at him again. All I could think about was our afternoon cuddle session in bed and the way he had gazed at me so unabashedly in adoration. I felt an overpowering need to listen to him tell one of his funny stories again. His Portuguese accent was sexy. I probably overdressed and practically ran over the wood planks to the big house. It did not escape me that I was acting like an infatuated teenager.

James, Maxine, Steve, and Mr. Daxter each already held a crystal of wine. Maxine and Steve had their heads together in conversation, discussing Steve's police station visit. James sat quietly eavesdropping, and from the bits of their conversation, it seemed everyone agreed that the police were making an accident into something more sinister. Maxine claimed that several river wanderers often made paranoid claims of being stalked by mystery people. Mostly, men felt stalked by women and women by men.

"Mentally ill," Maxine said. "That man was mentally ill."

Mr. Daxter nodded vigorously in agreement with her assessment.

Bruno stood at the small bar with several bottles of his family's wine. His eyes lit up as I entered the room, and I couldn't help smiling at him in response. Instant heat flooded my face as I took in his white collared shirt, unbuttoned at the neck, and nice fitted slacks. He was incredibly handsome. My eyes dropped to his hands on the bottle and glass as he slowly poured the wine, our wine. That little motion made me extremely hot. I stole a quick glance toward Steve, and he only just noticed me. He stood and went to fetch the glass of wine from Bruno, then delivered it to me. He leaned toward me, smiling. He leisurely admired my dress.

"You look radiant, sexy," he whispered.

I frowned at him, then went to sit in the love seat beside the leather wingback chair James had claimed. I expected Steve to take his former seat next to Maxine, but he followed me over and squeezed into the love seat with me. I felt his hand slide along the back of the settee behind my shoulders. He lightly touched my bare shoulder. I moved to shake him off, and he acted like he didn't notice. He leaned in close.

"I take it, this dress means you're ready to forgive me tonight?" he whispered.

Gad, that dress! It's the one I wore the first time we ended up in bed. How could I have forgotten that?

"Shall we wait for Aster?" James said suddenly. "I think she took something. She looked groggy. I tried to wake her an hour ago, but she was out of it."

"Oh, she's always on something and always late." Steve's deep voice hung close to my ear. He had leaned toward me like he always did, only now I wasn't so fond of his hovering proximity. "Let's not worry about her. Why don't we go ahead and start?"

Bruno had come around to sit directly across from me.

"Your son," he raised his glass toward Maxine, "my father. He loved the science of wine. At our winery in southern Brazil, the fermentation process occurs underground, in a climate-controlled basement. My father believed the key to success was a cold fermentation process. I bring you his life's work. He was proud of this batch of wine."

Maxine nodded and took a small sip.

"It's very nice. Sweet."

Everyone sipped and nodded.

"That is sweet. Is it sweetened with extra cane sugar?" James asked.

Bruno shook his head.

"Honey," Bruno said. "Our honey blends in Brazil provide intricate textures of flavor. Our father was diabetic and wanted to avoid using any extra sugar."

James smiled and took a deep swallow.

We all enjoyed the wine. Bruno spoke about the production on the family vineyard and the hills where they planted a select patch of grapes. Most of the wine they made came from purchased grapes, but it was the dream of Bruno's father to have a completely self-producing facility. That dream was within reach but needed a few more years to take root. Bruno fetched a fresh bottle from the table to recharge glasses as needed.

"I wonder what's taking Aster so long." James rubbed his hands nervously. "Are we going to wait for her? Don't you have messages to deliver from our father? A message for each of us. Is there one for me?"

Bruno swallowed and nodded.

"Please, tell me my message now," James said.

Bruno stiffened momentarily, then relaxed and poured more wine. He glanced briefly at me.

"He… he wishes you well, in life," Bruno said. "He regrets not knowing you and hopes for your happiness and success."

James clenched his lips together and sat back.

"What a wonderful message," James spat. "Thirty-three years, and he wishes for my happiness and success? Is that the same message he has for Aster and Alex too?"

"Now, James…" Maxine started.

"Oh, no." James was beet red, angry. "That's not the real message, is it? The real message is that he wishes for you and that winery down there to get funded with the Winters trust. That's the real message, isn't it! Isn't that what you came for?" James glanced at Mr. Daxter.

Mr. Daxter just about choked mid-sip of wine.

Steve shifted to a more upright position and glared at Bruno, ready to side with James. Bruno widened his eyes and shrugged.

"It is the truth." Bruno nodded. "I am here on my father's request, his dying request. He would like his share of the trust to go to his wife, my mother, so that the family can keep the winery from collapsing. It was his dream to leave the legacy of a winery. We would need the money to keep it going." Bruno nodded at James. "But he also wanted to send a message of love and forgiveness and regret for not knowing his other children."

Steve chuckled and settled back. He dropped a hand on my leg, and I moved. The look in his eye told me he had the wrong idea, he thought we were playing cat and mouse, flirting. He caressed my thigh, and I pushed his hand aside. He just grinned at me. He turned to Bruno.

"Unfortunately, the marriage certificate you provided is just a piece of paper, right, Dax?" Steve said. "Scribbled out by who knows who, who knows where? And the more recent version, well, how legal is that one, Dax?"

Mr. Daxter coughed. "Yes, well, that one is legal," he said.

Bruno nodded slightly.

"Let's not get too far ahead of ourselves, though," Mr. Daxter waved a hand toward him. "Unfortunately, your parents got the official seal a little too late for it to make a difference here. In order to pass his trust to a wife, that bond would need to be at least six months old, and the date on the official document is barely a month ago."

Bruno shook his head. "They were married for twenty-six years."

"You'll still receive some of the trust," Mr. Daxter said. "His name is clearly on your official birth certificate, and the way Henry Winters wrote things out, you'll enjoy a similar split with the other grandchildren. Unless there's an acceptable marriage with an heir, then things get divided a little differently."

"You're kidding!" Steve sat up again.

James stared hotly. "Nobody knew Bruno existed until last May when Richard started with the letters. Doesn't that sound suspicious? How do we know the marriage isn't fake, or the birth certificate? He never let Maxine know about his *family* down in Brazil, how do we know this isn't some sort of scam?"

"That isn't true," Bruno narrowed his eyes at James. He turned to Maxine. "He sent a letter, many years ago, more than one. And my mother's family, they tried to reach out, several times. They sent you presents, important gifts from the family. Gifts with meaning."

"Yes, I remember," Maxine said. "But I'm sorry, Bruno. Richard was very flighty back then, anxious and spur of the moment, an irresponsible young man, always needing an advance on his allowance. I now realize he must have matured and become a different man in those years. You must understand that the father you knew is not the son I remember. I'm sorry. I did not believe he had truly married or started a real family. I thought he was trying to solicit money. The truth is, we did not believe you or your mother existed, until last year, as James said."

Bruno's jaw tightened, and I was not pleased with Maxine in that moment. I suddenly stood and crossed the space to sit next to Bruno. I took his hand in mine and rubbed his back with my other hand other. He smiled weakly at me. Steve watched with an amused expression on his face.

"Of course, if we'd known about you sooner, we would have reached out," Maxine added. Her eyes met mine with an odd expression in them. Was that hostility?

Mr. Daxter coughed again. "The situation about marriages, and the clause, might make this whole conversation moot. Aster called me earlier and mentioned a potential fiancé, and now I learn that Steve and Amanda have decided to speed things up. Someone mentioned the potential for an heir in the works. You say you two are planning an immediate family." Mr. Daxter glanced between me and Steve.

"Amanda," Steve cleared his throat. "Please, you know me, optimistic. We can talk later."

Maxine quickly addressed Mister Daxter, "Everything is still being decided." She gave me weak smile.

I ignored Maxine and glared at Steve. "We will definitely talk later."

He fluttered his puppy eyes at me and gave me a flirty grin. Everyone was staring at us, and I was tempted to do something rude, like throw my wine in his face.

James suddenly stood up. He left the room mumbling something about fetching Aster. Every muscle on his face flexed tightly as he stomped away.

"Amanda?" Maxine said.

"Yes," I snapped.

I must have given her a hard look because she began clutching her chest. Her eyes appeared worried, and I immediately wiped whatever anger I had off my face. I gave her a reassuring nod and reached out to take her hand. She took the opportunity to grip mine. Her eyes pleaded with me, and my heart hurt for her. I certainly wanted things to go her way, but I also did not want to encourage Steve.

Before anything else was said, Aster meandered into the room with James at her heels. Her eyes were glazed over, and she laughed at us sitting there watching her. Bruno stood up and met her at the bar. He poured a fresh glass of wine and held it out to her. She took the bottle out of his hand instead and grinned wickedly before clumsily drinking from it.

Maxine let out an exasperated breath.

"Aster!" Mr. Daxter said. "Tell us about this fiancé you called about."

She gave him an amused look. "Everyone knows Chucky. He owns the mansion next door. His family is old money from Boston, just like you, Maxine, and you, Amanda." She chuckled at me.

"He's a drug dealer," James spat at Daxter, "and probably an addict, that disqualifies him right off the bat, right?"

Mr. Daxter nodded. "As long as it's documented."

James grimaced at him.

"What does that mean?" Aster mumbled.

"A police record, or evidence of a hospital stay, or something of the sort."

Aster meandered toward the door carrying the bottle of wine.

"Is this all there is? Just wine and lawyer talk? People hating on me? Insulting my fiancé? You people deal with it. I'm going back to my room. I'll just take my portion of the wine with me."

"Don't you want to hear our father's dying message to you?" James snapped as he plopped back into his seat.

Aster laughed. "I'll pass. He never said nothing to me when he was alive, so why would I listen to him now that he's dead? Besides, I already got my message. I believe my little brother over there," she stared at Bruno, "snuck into my room and left a little card from my papa. You did, didn't you?"

Bruno nodded at her. "He wrote that card for you alone, personally, and I did not believe you would want to share it."

Aster stood still as a statue.

"I burned it. Did you do anything else in my room?" she asked softly.

Bruno reddened. "I did nothing else."

"Are you sure? Because it looks like someone fiddled with my things."

Bruno shook his head, face red, eyes blinking.

Aster turned her eyes on James, Steve, and also me. "Stay away from my stuff, people. I've got someone on my side now, and I won't be bullied."

"Oh, Aster, please," Maxine gasped. "No one is bullying you."

"You got that right," she snapped, then flew from the room.

Everyone stayed silent for a few minutes after she left. I felt sorry for Bruno, his toast to his father was not going well. He seemed to take things in stride and returned to settle next to me.

"She's grieving," I told him.

"She's a troubled girl," Maxine corrected.

"She is crossing the line with her Chucky talk," James said. "I hope you aren't taking her seriously, Dax."

Perhaps we should fast forward her something, a nice cash amount, to allay her fears and calm her down," Steve added.

Mister Daxter nodded at him.

"All this talk, and all this wine, I'm afraid has done me in." Maxine placed a hand on her chest. "It's been a long day, and I'm emotionally exhausted. I think it's best if I retire." She nodded at me. "Amanda, would you help me to my room?"

What could I do? Everyone stood up, with Steve giving Maxine a helping hand. As I led Maxine down the hall, Steve followed close behind, hovering. Maxine gave him a stern wave of the hand. He looked me up and down once more before disappearing back toward the others. *Why did I wear that risqué dress?*

Maxine pulled me into her room and shut the door. She turned and clutched my hands.

"Amanda, you must marry Steve. For me, for my legacy, for you, and for your future children." Her words shot out rapidly. "You need to quickly get over this spat about those girls. That was nothing and has nothing to do with your love. Please, get over it fast, because I know you will, eventually, in the end, and if you wait too long, your future will not be as comfortable."

She pulled me further into the room.

"That lawyer is going to divide my entire life's fortune and hand equal amounts to every one of them without a qualm. They don't deserve it. It was the last thing Henry did to me, making that ironclad trust, and he did it to punish me. To put me back in my place."

"Maxine, I—"

"No, no. Let me finish," she insisted. "The longer you wait, the more certain my legacy will be ripped into pieces and scattered among the undeserving. James has always pushed to have it split between him and Steve, but I don't want James to get a cent of it. And God forbid that drug addict walks away with my sweat and tears. If you and Steve marry immediately, you can get pregnant right away, then together, you can claim it all. You only need a doctor's confirmation before the six-month waiting period on the trust expires. Richard's death certificate is dated just shy of a month ago, so that gives you five months to get preg—"

"Maxine!"

"The house will be in your name. I'll make it a wedding gift. It's the only thing I control," she said.

"Maxine."

"It's my legacy, it's your future. You will be angry at yourself for holding this grudge too long. Yes, I agree, he should not get off too easy, but too much is at stake here. And I know you two love each other, I have seen you together. You will forgive him, eventually, and take him back because you belong together. This house should be yours."

Maxine patted my hand, then she gripped my arms to make her point.

"You risk losing a grand fortune by dragging this out, and I can't... I don't want those others to get any of it. Punish him later, for me. Forgive him now, punish him later, for your children."

Her face was wrinkled in a mess of hurt. I'd never seen her so desperate. She finally let my arms go, and I slouched away from her.

"Is it because you barely know them, is that the problem? But what about James? What do you have against James? Is it because he's gay?"

Maxine eyes widened as her entire body cringed inward. "Of course not, I'm not a bigot. I don't care if he's gay. It's because he's not my real grandson. His mother was a whore who slept with everyone and destroyed my family. She broke my boys. She chased off Richard and then killed my Tommy in a car accident when he confronted her about James's real father, the gardener of all people. We fired him years ago, but James is the spitting image of him, and sometimes, it pains me to look at him. Their son will never get a cent of that trust, never! Just the thought infuriates me."

I sank down on her bed. That was so unexpected.

"Does James know?"

"Do you think I'd be so cruel that I'd tell him his mother was a whore who broke up the entire family by sleeping with random men, including Tom?" Maxine flinched. She stared at me, probably wondering if I had caught that slip of the tongue. "He can have a nice lump sum, but not a percentage of the assets. Not the trust, the company. The company must stay intact. If that lawyer divides up the trust, it will all be lost."

"What about Aster? She is your actual granddaughter, not me."

"She's a drug addict. I will not allow my fortune to be traded for a cheap fix. And God forbid her little threat about Chucky pans out. That man would love to stick it to me."

"What about Bruno?" I said softly. "Shouldn't Bruno's mother receive part of her husband's inheritance?"

Maxine opened her mouth but immediately shut it firmly. Her head hung down, and she laced her fingers together in her lap.

"If we can secure the trust with Steve and save the company, he can gift an amount to his late uncle's widow. He can invest in his cousin's winery," she said calmly. "Any other way would be chaos, Amanda. You have a tender heart, it's one of the many traits I love about you, but you don't understand the treachery at play."

Her old wizened eyes came up to capture mine.

"Bruno did not travel to America to deliver messages of goodwill. If that were the case, he would have come years ago, James is right about that. Bruno came here to steal the family fortune. Last year, when Richard tried to reconnect with me, it was clear his wine business was in financial trouble. Mark my words, his son wants the money, and I believe he'll even try to work through you to ensure that he gets it, just like the others."

I stood up and hugged my arms to my chest. "Oh, please, Maxine. How could he possibly work through *me* to get to *your* fortune?"

"By ensuring that you and Steve do not marry in time to alter the splitting of the trust."

She reached out a wavering hand to retrieve one of mine. She squeezed. Her whole body was shaking.

"It is a devious game at play, so please be careful. I may be an old woman, but I notice everything and am well acquainted with the ways of the world. Bruno would very much enjoy seducing you for his own purposes. He's a Latin lover, Amanda, and is aware of his appeal, so be careful around him. He realizes that his stake in the trust is jeopardized if someone marries and has an heir on the way. He isn't stupid. You and Steve are the closest to having that happen, and you threaten his plans. He would love to keep you and Steve apart."

I stared at her. "Did you and Steve orchestrate all this? For the trust. Are you using me?"

Oh, the devastation that passed onto her face. Her entire body sagged as if I punched her in the gut, and a flood of tears developed behind her eyes. She looked defeated, and I felt terrible.

"Oh, Amanda," she managed between hiccups. "Their poison has gotten to you."

She sobbed quietly into her hands, and I felt like an absolute monster. My arms snaked out to pull her close to me. *Why did I say that?* Maxine had been nothing but wonderful to me.

"All my life…" She faltered.

"Shh," I hushed. "I'm sorry for saying that."

She straightened up and wiped each eye.

"It's understandable, how you might jump to that conclusion with our recent guests," she said. "I'm happy you felt safe enough to share your fear with me. It tells me that our bond isn't completely tainted by this terrible week, and it tells me why you are still angry at Steve."

She pulled herself together and reset her steady eyes on me.

"Now, maybe, you understand why I kept the others at a distance. For years, the twins, and James, have been circling my doorstep like vultures, waiting to cash out. You will never understand it, but my heart breaks imagining the legacy my family built will go to people who are not my true family and care nothing for me. Steve is my only true grandson."

I was happy she was no longer crying, but I still felt uncomfortable.

"You're not being used, Amanda." She took my hand. "Don't lose sight of the fact that you fell in love *before* any of this was an issue. You chose to marry *before* the timer was set on that trust fund. Steve loves you, not for any other reason than that you are the perfect woman for him. He realizes he would be lucky to have you. And me too, I realize it. I love you like my own true blood. All my life I wished for a soul sister, and the moment we met and shared our first conversation, I knew that you were the dream granddaughter I always wanted. We share a kindred soul. Nothing would make me happier than to welcome you into my family, for you and Steven to have children, and to leave you kids with the gift of my entire legacy. I could go to my grave happy."

She babbled on and on about how Steve and I were perfect together. She reminded me of our many happy months together. She insisted that he had never been as ecstatic with another woman and he absolutely adored me. I didn't say a word, because I did not want to upset her. I checked her pulse and noticed her heart rate would not calm down. I fetched my phone, and we called the doctor again.

As I rummaged through her meds, I noticed she only had two beta blockers left in the container. Maxine did not know where the rest of them went, perhaps when she spilt them, they had all been lost. She did not know where James had put them when we had cleaned up.

The doctor insisted Maxine come to his house for the night, and Maxine agreed. It was not unusual; Maxine often stayed overnight at the doctor's house. They were old friends, and he lived just down the Garden Highway. We gathered a small overnight bag, then went out to tell the others. Maxine insisted Mr. Daxter drive her and James stay and enjoy more of the Brazilian wine with the rest of us.

Chapter 10

After watching Mr. Daxter drive off with Maxine, I strolled back to my bungalow alone. Her words had given me a terrible headache, and I began to doubt myself again. I've never been good with men, never able to read their true motivations, and often made terrible decisions, starting with that handsome professor when he convinced insecure, impressionable me that I was brilliant, beautiful, and the one woman he could not live without. It turns out that there were many brilliant young women he could not live without, and my heart had been shattered. The risky behavior he had coerced from me was not unlike the things Steve solicited from his own students.

After the professor came the grad student who loved *everything about me*, such as my apartment, home-cooked meals, hot showers, and the washing machine. I didn't realize he had moved into a rent-free situation until I requested that he sleep at his own place for a night.

And let's not forget the married man. The one who never mentioned he was married, or had children, or suffered instant amnesia in the presence of his wife. After six months of dating and a romantic balloon adventure where he presented me with a small engagement ring, he acted as if we were strangers when I bumped into him with his family one night. I spent several days wondering if his proposal to her had been as spectacular as the one he made to me in that hot air balloon. I also wondered how many girls were running around town with one of his rings on their fingers.

I really was *too freaking easy.*

Finally came Steve. Doting, romantic, wealthy, clever, funny, handsome, sexually satisfying Steve. And he came with a mother figure. A girlfriend, mentor, and cheerleader I never dreamed of, Maxine. She was right. She was the soul sister I never had. If I couldn't trust myself, I could at least trust her. Yes, she had a vetted interest in Steve and me and had been over the moon that we hit it off, but she wouldn't push me toward a man who was bad for me. *Would she?*

And she was probably right. I would probably forgive him eventually and take him back because *I was easy.* He'd keep telling me the S&M sex play was only a class exercise, and he'd solicit more students to assure me that it was *innocent*, not coercive, not real, and eventually, I'd believe him because guys like Steve knew that easy girls like me could be broken down by continuous repetition and persistence.

Someone was already in my bungalow, lounging on the sofa, playing with his cell phone. It took a moment to confirm that it was Steve, not Bruno. He leaped to his feet and met me in the middle of the small room with an impassioned embrace. He didn't ask, he pulled me roughly against his chest, and his spontaneous hug actually calmed me down embarrassingly easy. Yet, he definitely was being amorous, so I struggled. It was almost pointless because was strong.

"Steve, no."

He kissed me greedily and held my arms tightly at the wrist so I couldn't hit him or push him away. He chuckled, thinking the struggles were more sex play. The night was dark, and it felt familiar and normal to be struggling with him, so I didn't panic right away. He kissed my neck all the way down to my cleavage. I admit this was something I enjoyed in the past, even in the present. It felt nice to be wanted so passionately. He was a good kisser, and the way he touched me, like he couldn't help himself, made my blood speed up a tad, though there was something valuable missing. I got a hand free and pushed against his chest, not ready to accept my fate yet, but my resistance was feeble after Maxine's speech, and my *no, no, no's* were weak and unconvincing whispers, even to my own ears. He grabbed my hair and pulled the dress strap off my shoulder, frightening me.

I stomped on his toe with enough force for him to shout out and release me. I moved three feet away and wiped my mouth where he had assaulted me.

"This is ridiculous," he frowned. "You wear that dress, staring at me with your come-hither eyes, moan like a nymph in heat when I kiss you, then stomp on my foot! Is this your way of penalizing me for fucking a few young girls once upon a time? I'm sorry, Amanda. I've not been a saint in the past, but you need to stop this nonsense and get your ass in that fucking bed!" He pointed to my bedroom.

"No, it's over."

"It's not over. If it was, you would have given me back the ring."

"I threw it in your face!"

"And then you picked it up for safe keeping," he grinned. "Because it's not laying on the floor, is it? You're a fireball, and I love it, a sexual dynamo. Do you want me to man-handle you? Is that what you need? Do you want it rough, need to pretend you're resisting so it's not your fault? Is that what you want? That's your favorite game, isn't it?"

My eyelids fluttered. I hated that he had hit on a small truth. I shook my head. "No."

I turned around and opened the drawer to fetch his ring. I rummaged around, but it wasn't there. *Where's my ring?* He was suddenly behind me, pushing me up against the desk with his entire body. I felt his large hard male appendage push its way between my buttocks. He had pushed my dress up and gripped my hips roughly.

"No."

His hands came around to the front of my dress, and they eagerly grabbed my breast, pinching harshly, then massaging soothingly. He panted in my ear, extremely turned on. He had done all of these things before, more than once, and those times, I had wanted it, ended up begging him to continue, but not this time. I struggled, but the movements only excited him more. His mouth was on my neck, kissing, biting, sucking, whispering loving, then shocking comments in turn.

"No!"

He spun me violently to face him and wedged himself between my legs. His eyes were dark and staring at the one taunt nipple he'd exposed. He licked his lips and looked into my eyes with a dark, dangerous, hungry expression. There was nowhere for me to go.

He suddenly went slack. His grin disappeared, and his grip loosened. He stumbled two steps away from me with confused muddled eyes.

"Are you crying?"

I was crying.

"You're crying."

The tears streamed down my face.

"God, Amanda, I... I... I-Is this real crying? Are you really crying?"

He backed up even more, pulling his legs and arms and hands into his body.

"I told you no," my voice was weak.

His face became a grimace of anger. His chest heaved with the task of breathing. "Okay," he nodded vigorously. "I... I'm sorry, I thought..."

We stood in silence, and a coldness descended on us.

"I want you to go."

"I'm not going anywhere," he said softly. "I won't touch you again, but I'm not going to leave you alone tonight. Not tonight."

"Why?" I stared helplessly at him.

"You might be in danger," he whispered. "Aster. She's unhinged, not right in the head. She did something to Alex, or she got Chucky to do something, I'm almost certain of it. And I think... I think you're in danger. So, I'm not going to leave you alone."

I felt so cold.

The funny thing is, at that moment, I wanted him to hug me. To feel the comfort of the familiar arms I had lost. And I wanted to hug him too, to make him feel better. His upset face, at the mistake he had made, crushed me. We had done those things before, not exactly like that, but similar, and it had always ended up spectacular for us.

"I'll sleep on the couch. And please, please don't go on any walks tonight. Stay inside where I can protect you. In the morning, I'll make the announcement about us. I'll tell Maxine and make it stick, if that's what you want. I'll accept it, that it's o-over."

He choked a little on that last word. He swallowed.

"Then, you'll be safe." He turned his face away from me.

He lay snoring on the couch, and I couldn't sleep. Part of me wanted to wake him up and make up, and the other part wanted to run away. I kept expecting Bruno to show up, but he must have noticed Steve follow me home. Perhaps he waited for Steve to leave but saw that he didn't. What did Bruno think about Steve sleeping in my bungalow?

And what was up with Bruno? *Did he steal my engagement ring?* He must have.

After Steve had brewed up warm tea, I sat at the desk searching all around for the ring, but it was gone. I distinctly remember putting it directly back into the drawer, right in that divot for pencils. So, it was not lost, it was stolen.

When did Bruno take it? *When he retrieved his shirt!* I shut my eyes. I was such an idiot.

Seven and a half carets in diamonds, and that big blue beautiful stone, all held together with a special alloy of seventy-five percent gold and twenty-five percent silver. *Not a single drop of copper*, Steve had bragged, *only precious metals for my girl.* It was one of a kind. Worth at least a forty grand.

Was Bruno that desperate for money? *A Latin lover, he knows his appeal,* Maxine's voice echoed in my ear.

He strutted around in those tight shorts, shirtless and preening without a care in the world. Lighting my cigarette like the hero in a dreamy old movie. He made sure to have a poignant moment in front of me, tearing up. He fed me sweet wine mixed with romantic exciting stories of youthful adventure and another with a love at first sight theme. Then, he literally carried me to bed and automatically did every single thing that popped into my brain. Who did that except movie men and book boyfriends? He was fiction, pure fiction. *Be careful, Amanda.* I was too easy!

Steve snored innocently in sleep. So cuddlable. I felt guilty. I betrayed him, even if we were broken up. Now, I realize, my anger at him had really been at myself. Anger that I had been *that girl*, like the one from his video clip, maybe I still was, and someday, she might be me, running to a Steve to validate her.

Would she fall for her Steve just because of his wealth and position, and because he brought her flowers and complimented her tirelessly? Would she keep running to him, over and over again, and never stop to check if she really, truly, loved him, or if the relationship was rooted in anything real? Would she ever admit that the entire relationship was just a beautiful façade, propped up to look authentic because a little old lady urged her along and assured her that they were perfect for each other?

Admittedly, our entire relationship revolved around Maxine. Days of me being a companion to Maxine followed by nights of Steve. He'd dive into my world after dusk with romantic overtures that led to those passionate nights. We never had a fight, because we never had a real conversation. It had been man, woman, flirting, wooing, and passion on repeat, with entertaining Maxine in between.

The inside of the little bungalow was getting claustrophobic, and I needed to get some air. I knew I promised to stay inside, but I couldn't take it any longer and slipped out the side door. I snuck around to the porch to breathe and heard a *hoot-hoot*.

I spotted the little devil watching me, her eyes shone in the slight light of the crescent moon. Was she really female, or did Bruno invent that bit to amuse me? The owl shivered before flying off. She'd never flown off with me watching before, spreading her wings and soaring into the dark sky looking magnificent. That girl was not afraid of anything.

I wondered if she had a baby in that tree. How lucky for her, a baby would be a beautiful miracle. Maybe two babies, a handsome boy and a cute girl, Chase and Colette, both small and cuddly. For the past half year, it's all I'd been thinking about, *babies, babies, babies…* but now, I need to get babies out of my head. Because having babies on the brain made easy girls like me make stupid decisions about idiot men, like the one on my couch. *Gad!* A standard daytime fantasy flooded my head. Steve playing the part of a doting, charming father holding our little baby, cooing to it and looking at me with his seductive eyes, hoping to make another one. I forcefully blanked it out, completely annoyed with myself.

The sky was overcast, and the night extremely dark, and an overpowering urge overtook me. I wanted to peek into the owl's nest and look for an owlet. If she really was female, then she must be a mother, why wouldn't she be? The urge to climb up to that hidey hole was overpowering. The yard crew always kept a small ladder by the rope swing, and it might be tall enough to reach the hole in the oak tree. I wouldn't go near the outer edge of the property, so there was no real danger.

I snuck down to Maxine's patio to grab her large camp light. A peek into the den told me that no one was up. The wine glasses had been cleared away, and the house felt quiet. I turned and crept onto the property to find the ladder. The air cooled dramatically on the lawn, and water noises from the river sounded louder. I let out a calming breath.

Suddenly, there was an odd noise between me and the bungalow. I paused to listen. Were those footsteps? Was someone sneaking slowly in my direction? My heart started pumping.

I hurried in the opposite direction toward the pool house. I moved rapidly in that direction.

The footsteps followed me, also speeding up.

The night began to close in on me, and my pace turned into a speed walk.

The footsteps sped up with mine.

"I'll get you," a voice growled.

Who was that? Panic developed in my breast, and I increased my speed again.

The footsteps also increased in speed.

"Leave me alone," my voice came out horse, broken.

"I've been waiting for you."

"Chucky?" I gasped in a strained voice. Why had he been waiting for me?

You are in danger, Steve's voice echoed in my ear.

He chuckled. "You know who it is, girly."

I paused for only a second, then I high-tailed it to the pool house. Big mistake, he had booked it up the back patio and now stood between me and the main house. He searched into the darkness with his big round eyes bulging. Luckily, I stood in the corner under a tree, hidden from him.

"You can't get away from me, girly!" he hissed gleefully.

He quickly leaped down to the pool area, which prompted me to skid into the gravel drive and start running away. Blood pounded in my ears. Stomping footsteps trailed behind me. There was no way I could outpace him on the road, so I ducked onto his property and zigzagged through his crooked garden. My attempts to stay quiet and move stealthily in the shadows were feeble. Every sound echoed like a cannon boom to me. I longed to turn on the camp light but knew he'd see it easily. Terror engulfed me as his cursing voice carried over the air and slipped into my ear. What did he want? Why had he been waiting for me? Had Steve been right? Was this Aster's doing? I recalled her disgusted sneer in the bar the other night.

You are too easy. She hated me.

The little trail to that beach miraculously materialized, drawing me in. I knew the trail well, and after a while, the footsteps behind me faded away. My pace slowed to a walk, and my ears remained alert, taking in every swish of leaves, every tinkle of water. My own heavy breathing scared me, and my vision blurred with the moist air. I found my favorite small half-moon of sand and hurried to the far side to sit in the foliage.

It took several minutes, or hours, for my racing blood to ebb. My eyes stared across the sandy beach expecting to see Chucky emerge at any moment. Flickering shadows kept my muscles tense and nerves on edge. I scooted back into the brambles, tucking myself under the branch of a small tree, trying not to make so much noise with every exhale. I gripped the camp light, my weapon, then lay flat on the ground for the rest of the night, convinced I was about to die. Somehow, I fell asleep.

Chapter 11

The sunrise altered my perspective considerably, and my attitude took a one hundred and eighty degree turn around. As the shadows morphed into normal leaves, vines, sand, and water of the river, I no longer felt the danger that had consumed me in the dark. I felt silly for hiding on the cold dark beach and irritated with my sore muscles and bug-bitten legs. I stumbled through the foliage, following the trail back to Chucky's house. I skirted his lawn where it met the high riverbank and stepped through the bushes onto the manicured grass of Maxine's large property.

Several police officers meandered along the edge of the bank, looking down toward the river. Officer Shane Bane glanced up just as I recognized him. His mouth drooped opened, and he started moving toward me. The others stopped to watch.

"Is that her?" one of them called out.

"Miss O'Hare!" Officer Bane waved to me, grinning happily. "Are you alright?"

My arrival instigated a plethora of activity. Policemen converged on me, and first James, then Bruno, then Steve rushed out of the house. Officer Bane cleared a path and led me toward the patio. Steve leaped down the steps and grabbed me into a tight hug, squeezing me. He kissed my cheeks and forehead, then moved a step back but did not let me go. He held me in a loose, one-armed embrace.

"Thank God you're okay." His chest heaved in relief.

James shot me a pleased smile from a reasonable distance. "Geez, Amanda, you had us all worried. We thought the worst."

Bruno stood a few feet away with a somber expression. His lips were pressed together in an odd way. I didn't want to look at him. *Did he take my ring? Did he try to seduce me?*

I relayed what had happened in a statement to Officer Bane. Chucky had been wandering Maxine's property, then started chasing me. Who knew what he wanted, but his stalking felt dangerous, so I ran into the brush and hid on a small beach. I apologized for scaring everyone.

Officer Bane jotted it all down in his little notebook.

"No need to apologize. It looks like your instinct to run was a good one," he nodded.

"What do you mean?"

"Your neighbor," Officer Bane told me. "Chuck Collins is missing. We can't find him anywhere, and we really need to speak with him."

Police officers were everywhere. Inside Maxine's house, over at the Chucky's house, walking along the levy wall. I glanced at the guys and only James would tell me anything.

"Aster overdosed," he said softly. "They think someone, Chucky, gave her something bad."

Steve scowled at him and began guiding me away.

"I'm going to take her home and clean her cuts. You two stay away."

We were in the small den of my bungalow sitting close together on the sofa. Steve found the first aid kit, and he used two large fingers to rub antibiotic cream on every single cut and bite mark on my legs. He took his time.

Earlier in the morning, Steve went into the main house searching for me and proceeded to wake everyone up. That's when he found Aster laying in her bed with the mint tin open, pills spilled across the bedspread and a near-empty bottle of that Brazilian wine sitting on her night table. She had been dead for hours, he said, but he immediately called for an ambulance and the police. When the extra police arrived to look for me, the detective noticed some of the pills on Aster's bespread were odd, and they wondered if she had taken something new and experimental. An officer was sent to question Chucky, but he was missing.

"James and Bruno were acting strange. They all but accused me of doing something to you," Steve said. "I can't believe that prick, James. He actually told the police that I threw you into the river because you broke up with me. They were ready to cuff me. And Bruno, he was so tight-lipped, he would barely say a word to anyone."

Besides holding hands, Steve rarely touched me unless it was a lead-up to something more, and he was taking his time with his first aid, being gentle and careful. This was a new experience for us, having him attend to me like this. His tongue was clenched between his lips as he concentrated, and I giggled at him. He caught my eye and frowned at me.

"This isn't funny. I asked you not to go outside last night."

"Sometimes I need air. I was feeling—"

"Guilty."

"Guilty?"

"Guilty." His eyes were stern.

"Why would I feel guilty? Do you think I did something to Aster now?"

He shook his head. "No, not about anything like that."

"Then what?"

"Guilty about him, Bruno," he said.

My face gave me away.

"I'm not an idiot, Amanda. I've seen the glances, the way his eyes follow you, and the way he's tried to flirt with you, flaunting his pecker in those wet shorts. He's cute and young, and I get it. Getting excited about a cute young person, especially when you're mad at me, I get it. Don't worry, if you fantasized about him with that toy of yours, I forgive you. Did you actually kiss him?"

My face flushed quickly.

"I can forgive you for that too, for kissing him. I get it. You were angry at me, maybe wanted to get back at me, and he probably came on strong..."

Steve threw the ointment back into the first aid kit, upset. He simmered just below the surface. I kept my mouth shut.

"The way he acted when you went missing made everything obvious, that you must have actually kissed him and you were feeling guilty. Is that why you were crying last night? It is, isn't it?"

He took out a bandage and tried to make it stick to the lubricated wounds. Finally, he had to wipe off some of the ointment and use a different one to make it stick.

"Yes, I'm upset, but it doesn't really mean anything to me, Amanda, because what we have is love. I love you." His eyes stared into mine. "You're my girl."

I swallowed guiltily.

"Don't give the ring back," he said softly, making my heart pound. "I love you."

I swallowed again. "What do you love about me?"

"God, everything. I love that you're kind and sweet and so patient with Maxine. She loves you, and she never gets along with anybody. You're so perfect with that old woman. The sparkle in her eye since you've been here. You make our dinners fun, I've never been interested in her prattle, but you, you keep the conversation going. You listen to people. You're an angel, a Godsend. Just what she needed to see out her last years."

Maxine, Maxine, Maxine.

"And after Maxine dies, what will you love about me then?"

He stiffened. His mouth drooped for a moment. "What do you mean?"

"I mean, without Maxine, what do you love about me?"

He blinked at me and chuckled. "Well, you're extremely sexy, we click, you can't deny it, we have great chemistry, off-the-charts sex. And that has nothing to do with Maxine."

"The girl in your video was also sexy," I said. "And cute, and young, and it looked like you were going off the charts. Are you going to give up that hobby, or are you expecting me to do some of those things? Will I have a choice? Did that girl have a choice? It looked like maybe she had changed her mind."

He pressed his lips together and backed up. "It was a ridiculous class activity, Amanda. Why are you blowing it out of proportion? She was acting out her part, trying to understand something. *Jesus*, Amanda, you talked to her on the phone. I didn't pressure her to do those things. It's nothing like what you experienced. I do not bully my students with grades, or promises, or anything else. Everyone is an adult, and nobody is coerced in the least. Not one person was forced to do anything they didn't want to do."

"Does the entire class participate together, or is it a one-on-one activity with the professor?"

He didn't answer.

"Did you take any of them out to dinner?"

He scoffed.

"Answer me," I demanded.

"Sometimes I treat students to dinner, especially when they've done something great and I'm rewarding them, celebrating with them. I enjoy propping up my students. Yes, some of the students in that class hit milestones, and yes, I took a few out to dinner."

"Did any of those milestones involve your *class activity*?"

He closed his mouth again and narrowed his eyes. "You insist on making me out to be a monster," he growled.

I didn't say anything.

"Are you going to marry me or not?"

"Right now, I don't know how I could," I said.

"You're going to lose your chance here, Amanda. Think very carefully about what you want because there's going to be a point of no return, and you'd better decide what you want before we get there."

He slammed the first aid kit closed and stomped to the back door. He punched the wall before opening the door, leaving a dent in the drywall. He turned hot, angry eyes on me. Then, they went soft, and I watched him blink away his emotions as his sad puppy eyes looked longingly at me. *Why do I feel like the cruel one?*

Chapter 12

The afternoon slipped away as I caught up on lost sleep. I woke groggy, hungry, and thirsty, and the scratches on my legs burned. I examined all the angry red lines before crawling out of bed. In my dream, Steve had turned out to be Mack McKinzie, my professor from college, and he was sincerely sorry for all the confusion, he actually did love me. In my dream, he was crying and apologizing for everything, but he had Steve's face, and in the hall waiting for his office hours, three other girls sat quietly watching, and that box from the hall closet sat on the ground at their feet.

I stumbled into my living area and noticed them right away, James and Bruno in chaise lounge chairs on my patio, talking and drinking what looked like iced tea. They both noticed me at the same time and stood to stare at me.

I pushed the sliding door open.

"Hi!" James exclaimed. "I hope we didn't wake you.

Bruno wore the classic Winters' puppy dog eyes.

"What are you guys doing out here?"

"We were worried about you," Bruno said. "We wanted to be near when you woke."

"Chucky is still missing," James added. "It made us both feel better sitting out here."

Bruno nodded. "It's also better for us, to know you are safe."

"Has Steve gone home?" I asked.

They both nodded.

"And Maxine?"

"She's coming home later," James said. "The doctor took her to his clinic for tests."

We stood staring at each other for a few quiet minutes.

"Well, I'm famished," I confessed. "I need to get something to eat."

James drove us down the winding Garden Highway to Swabbies for fish tacos and to enjoy the live music. Swabbies often hired cover bands, and the entertainment for that evening happened to specialize in seventies and eighties rock ballads. We meandered to a table close to the river, and James diverted to the outdoor bar to order drinks instead of waiting for the waitress. Bruno took the opportunity to cover my hand with his.

"I am glad to see you safe," he said.

"I'm sorry, Bruno…" I took my hand back and hid it under my arm.

Bruno looked wounded.

I needed to change the name in my WIP again, or perhaps, I could recover the section I deleted. *Gad*, that whole thriller was a disaster. Perhaps I should just chuck it with all my other failed stories. Maybe I wasn't meant to be a novelist. Maybe I was only a ghostwriter.

James returned with bottles of beer.

"It's shocking about Aster," I blurted.

They both solemnly agreed, and the waitress dropped by to take our orders. She openly flirted with Bruno. His sparkling eyes were hard to resist. In fact, several women had noticed him, but he only had eyes for me. I did my best to ignore them.

"She was eating the pills in her tin like they were mints," I continued. "Do you know what any of them were? She offered me a sample at the Firehouse the other night."

James shrugged his shoulders. "Probably Xanax or something similar."

They had minimal information about Aster. The police had gone through her things and discovered a small bag of white powder, probably cocaine, and the tin containing white pills in three different sizes. The news about Aster had put Maxine over the top with her blood pressure, and the doctor insisted she stay at his clinic so he could keep an eye on her. James kept shaking his head as he relayed the information. His face and neck had turned red again.

"I knew she was abusing what Chucky gave her." He looked away. "But I hated her and didn't care to step in." He massaged his brow.

"Oh, James." I reached over to rub his back. "Everyone watched her abusing drugs, and no one could have controlled her. None of us had a clue what she was used to, or that she'd go overboard. I mean, I didn't really know her at all, and I understand that you didn't, either."

James shook his head, "I need a moment."

He stood up and walked away. He headed toward the stage, keeping his face toward the band. Poor James, what a devastating week for him, losing two siblings and a father. Of course, he hadn't known any of them well, but still. Bruno lost them too. I found him staring at me with a wide, observant expression.

"I think we should go to a hotel," he said.

I scoffed.

"No," he said. "That is not what I mean. What I mean is… this family is not normal. It isn't safe in that house. Even James, yes, he seems sad, but he carries a tremendous amount of anger inside of him, and he is strange. I found him outside your door, perhaps he was trying to open it, and that is why I insisted on sitting with him on your porch. He should not be trusted."

I glanced toward James.

"You're saying I can't trust him? He might be the only one I can trust."

Bruno frowned. "You don't trust me?" he whispered.

"Did you steal my engagement ring?" I asked.

Oh, the face on Bruno! He definitely took my ring. He closed his mouth into a crease, and his eyes flicked away shamefully. He stiffened in his seat.

"It wasn't his to give you," he said.

What did that even mean?

"It wasn't yours to take," I said.

His eyelids were fluttering.

"Look, Bruno," I said. "I'm going through a bad breakup, and I'm confused, not thinking right. I'm sorry for what happened between us, but it was a one-time thing, a slip-up. It isn't anything more than that. We should just be happy it didn't go too far."

The image of his young fit body suddenly flashed in my head. It hadn't been me who stopped things the other afternoon, it had been Bruno keeping his promise. He had pulled me against his rock-hard muscles and held me while we both fell asleep. Then, I recalled those sweet moments when we just talked, like on the bench in Old Town, when he had calmed me so easily in the middle of a storm. The cascade of emotions rushing through my system was hard to interpret, and I tried to shake them away.

"I want my ring back. I need to either return it, or I need to… I need to decide what I'm going to do. Either way, I want my ring back. I don't care if you need the money, it's my ring, and you stole it from me. Have you stolen anything else?"

Bruno's nostrils flared. "Are you still thinking about accepting him? He's a liar. He'll always lie to you."

"Haven't you lied to me?"

His anger mounted, but he managed to contain himself.

"I've never lied to you, I never would. I am not like the rest of this family. My side of the family is honest, hard-working people. These people here, they are snakes."

"But you are a thief," I said. "And you are after the money too, aren't you? Is that why you're trying to interfere in my relationship with Steve? Worried about your inheritance like the rest of them? Did you seduce me for that purpose? I want my ring back."

"It's not his."

"It's not yours."

"It means nothing to him or them."

"He designed it out of love for me, and it means a lot to him, and to me."

"He's a liar."

Bruno leaned over the table. His eyes flashed with emotion, and there was no denying it, they were beautiful and quickened my heart. He clenched one hand into a fist, and all the muscles in his forearm flexed. But unlike Steve, his anger didn't scare me.

"He did not design that ring. That ring is the Paraiba Heart. It contains the largest stone my great grandfather ever dug from our family mine. The ring was designed years ago, in Brazil, a triumph, and it was sent to my father's mother in a pledge to bond our families."

He used a finger to point to the table to make his points.

"My grandparents sent that ring and a collection of three silver spoons in the pledge. Those spoons were the blood and sweat of my family. The last of the silver that served as our only collateral when my ancestors struggled with the mine. And the minerals, that blue tourmaline in particular, the money from our family mine, this is what funded my father's dream."

He calmed a bit and sank into his chair.

"Not a penny came from this family. But the wine business drained my mother's dowry, and she is now left with nothing if the winery goes under. So yes, I have come for the money... the money my father always promised my mother's family."

My heart was pounding.

"And I've also come for the ring and the spoons. These people rejected us in Brazil and should have returned those spoons and the ring with their rejection. Instead, they take and take with no acknowledgment or reciprocation, heartless and greedy, lying about everything and not caring for each other at all. I have never seen such coldness in a family. I feel my life is fragile with these people."

His eyes had gone completely dark, and he was very upset. But he took a couple of deep breaths and got himself settled somewhat. His eyes locked with mine for an instant before he stood up.

"I need to walk away for a moment as well."

His eyes were wounded as he stared at me, and I could see moisture pooling in them. I felt terrible with an overpowering urge to run to him and hug him.

"Yesterday," he whispered, "that was not a seduction. That was a happiness I never imagined I'd find, least of all here. I felt safe with you." He walked rapidly away, toward James and the stage.

What to do?

Every fiber of my being wanted to rush after him. Deep inside, though we barely just met, it seemed like we knew each other. I truly felt like I could trust him. Bruno felt ten times more trustworthy than Steve. Even in his anger, I wasn't afraid of him.

I decided to follow him, but a man at the bar stepped in front of me. Red hair, transparent eyes, tall and lean, he was one of Steve's many friends, standing next to the wooden pirate statue. Most of Steve's friends were just slightly creepy, all of them flirts who constantly boasted about themselves. If I remembered correctly, this one was a professional cyclist or something. When our eyes met, he gave me a charming smile and opened his arms for a hug.

"Amanda," he grinned and looked around. "I thought that was you. That wasn't Steve, was it?"

"It wasn't," I said sharply. "It was his cousin. Steve isn't here."

"Oh?" His eyes creased. "Hey, are you okay? You look like you might need a shoulder to cry on."

I shook my head and looked past him for Bruno and James.

"Is that James?"

"Yes, it is," I pushed past him. "I'm sorry, George, but I'm not in the mood to chat. I need to clear something up."

I continued past him and made my way to James and Bruno. Both of them had gotten their emotions under control, and they welcomed me between them. James glanced over my shoulder toward our table.

"Looks like our tacos have arrived," he announced. "Hey, is that George Johnson?"

"Yes, it is," I said.

James left to say hello to George, leaving me to face Bruno as a slow rock ballad began. Several couples met on the uneven dirt floor to sway in each other's arms. After a moment, I reached for Bruno's hand and pulled him out toward the dancers with me. He reluctantly followed. His hand felt warm, and the scent from his body was musky.

"I'm sorry," I whispered softly. "For accusing you back there. Steve told me that he designed the ring. He told me a beautiful story, and I believed him. Up until the last couple of weeks, I was in love with him and never imagined he'd lie about anything. Our world seemed perfect."

He nodded, not meeting my eye.

"It's been hard for me to accept some of what I learned, but I need to trust the evidence, not the stories."

He nodded, still not meeting my eye.

"I…" my voice was barely a whisper. "I never imagined anything like yesterday, either."

That got his eyes to meet mine. We stopped moving, and I couldn't breathe. His gaze melted my insides. I moved slightly away, and now it was my turn to have trouble looking at him.

"But I'm coming out of a very serious relationship here, and I'm working through some issues with it. And you're coming out of losing your father. We should be careful reading too much into this… this attraction we feel. We're both at emotional low points in our lives, and… and I'm sorry, but I'm not thinking straight and maybe neither are you."

He stiffened and pushed one hand into his pocket. He pulled out the ring, the Paraiba Heart. He pushed it into my hand and leaned close to whisper into my ear.

"Take it. Wear it if you like. Wear it for him, or wear it for me. Either way, it is yours if you want it. You can decide where it belongs. You can decide who is the honest one."

He walked away and joined James at the table. My heart pounded in my chest as I watched him walk away. I didn't want to lose the ring, so I slipped it on my finger for safe keeping. I was not going to give that ring back to Steve, but I was not wearing it for him, either. I was keeping it safe for Bruno.

Why did it hurt so much to watch him walk away?

Chapter 13

Maxine laughed in the den with Kira, her nurse. They enjoyed fancy takeout bubble tea. Kira jumped up the moment we entered the room, obviously waiting for our return so that she could leave. She pointed out a new medical container on the side table.

"Okay, now be careful with them," Kira smirked at James. "All of her meds are better organized, so we won't lose them so easily."

"So, my organization is to blame for the lost meds?" James asked her.

Maxine tutted as Kira left.

"Steve didn't dine with you?" Maxine noted. "The detective is coming. He wants to talk to everyone."

She suddenly spotted the ring on my finger, and her eyes danced with joy. James noticed her happy face and glared at the ring. He saw it earlier but hadn't said a word about it, but now he let his animosity shine through. Bruno only meandered aimlessly around the room, not sitting. He stood at the bookshelf silently perusing the titles with his hands tucked into his armpits. He hadn't said much to me after handing over the ring.

"Amanda, why don't you give Steve a call? Tell him about the detective. He should be here any minute now, and I assured him we would all be here." Maxine smiled at me.

"I can text him," James said. "I've been texting with him for the past hour."

James had been texting Steve for the past hour. That was news to me. I exchanged glances with Bruno, and he also seemed surprised. We sat in silence for several minutes and heard the car in the drive. We waited for the doorbell. When it rang, no one moved, so I did the honors and answered the door.

Detective Allen wore a corduroy tan jacket with patches on the sleeves. Although he was clean-shaven, a hint of roughness threatened to emerge along his chin, and his eyebrows were a bushy mess. He nodded and waved a hand back to the squad car in the drive. I spotted Officer Bane with his partner.

"They're just going to do a little look around before the light completely fades," he said.

He brushed the bottom of his shoes vigorously on the boot scrapper before coming in. I led him into the den and made the introductions. He nodded at everyone but did not take a seat. He flipped open a small computer pad and placed it on the coffee table.

"You'll all be happy to hear that we picked up Charles Collins earlier this evening." He glanced at me. "He's being questioned at the station as we speak. He admitted to chasing you, but denies threatening you. He claims that he thought you were Aster Winters."

I scoffed. "He was quite menacing, and he was threatening."

The detective paused to look at his computer tablet.

"His description of events matches the information you gave Officer Bane this morning."

He shifted his gaze to Maxine, then back at his tablet.

"He claims to have played an ongoing game of hide and seek with Aster in the dark, among other things." He shifted uncomfortably. "He admits giving her a low dosage mood stabilizer, but nothing else. We found several samples of that stabilizer in her tin, along with a few mints. But we also found something else. There were several samples of Atenolol."

James glanced at Maxine. He quickly sank back into his seat. His movement didn't go unnoticed by the detective.

"Anything you'd like to add, Mr. Winters?"

"No," James said quickly. "Well, it's just… Maxine takes Atenolol. Sparingly, but there's some in the house."

The detective turned to Maxine.

"Is this medication kept in a secure location?"

"Oh sure. I keep it in my room." Maxine nodded. "And a little sample in my purse. It's organized, all secure."

"Locked up?" the detective asked.

"Locked up? Whatever for?" She gave a short chuckle.

"Your granddaughter's overdose wasn't caused by anything Mr. Collins supplied. She actually died from an extremely high percentage of beta blockers in her system. They caused her heart to fail."

That news shocked everyone. Maxine glanced down at her hands, and James gripped the arms on his chair. Only Bruno appeared calm, relaxed. He watched in aloofness as Maxine fidgeted.

"Aster wasn't a toddler," Maxine said firmly. "She was an addict. Locks were not going to keep her out of my medicine cabinet." Her face looked strained.

"May I see your medicine cabinet?"

At that moment, Steve burst into the room. He glanced around and stopped to eye the detective harshly. After a moment, his eyes stopped on me and went right to my left hand and the ring on my third finger. His mouth twitched into a slight smile before he turned away. He walked up to the detective and stuck out his hand in greeting, then moved to stand next to Maxine. He casually placed a hand on the back of her chair in a protective manner. His eyes touched mine one more time before settling on the detective.

"Why do you need to see my grandmother's medicine cabinet?" he demanded.

"As I revealed a moment ago, your cousin Aster overdosed on beta blockers, high blood pressure medication, and I would like to confirm that there are similar pills kept in the house."

"You don't need to see her personal medicine cabinet," Steve said sharply. "Her health and medical care are confidential, privileged, it's nobody's business. If you'd like to know the exact brand of high blood pressure meds in the house, we can tell you. Or you can tell us which brand you're looking for, and we can confirm, yes, we have some in the house, or no, there isn't any that we know of."

Maxine beamed at Steve. He was her hero, and I was impressed with him too. He sensed her discomfort and knew just what to do. Goodness, I was proud of him. *He'd stand next to me too, to protect me, just like that.* His protective nature was definitely one of his attractive qualities. The detective nodded slightly and fiddled with his computer pad.

"That's fair," the detective said. "Did the Atenolol come from the dispensary at Natomas?"

"That's where we fill most of her prescriptions." Steve nodded.

"Can you tell me if there might be other medications Aster may have wanted?"

"Such as what?" Steve stared down at the detective. "Tell us what you're looking for, and we can tell you if it is a prescription medication here. But one thing I am not going to let you do, I am not going to let you invade Maxine's privacy by perusing her medicine cabinet. Nor am I going to rattle off every med this old lady is on without cause. She has a right to privacy. If you have a good reason, or a warrant, then we'll speak about it again."

The detective nodded, not looking up. He raised his hand.

"Of course," he acknowledged each of us in turn, tapping his finger on his pad. "But a word of caution, Mr. Winters. Our crime scene team insists there are two sets of footprints out along the levy, indicating quite a shuffling match at the place Alex fell into the beaver's dam. I'm aware you were informed of it at the station. I wonder if everyone here was informed of that."

He stared at Steve, sizing him up, and Steve widened his stance. The detective perused his tablet again.

"Another interesting curiosity, why would a drug addict swipe beta blockers and leave Xanax and oxycodone when given a choice? Can you tell me if those medications are all kept in the same location?"

Steve took a step toward the detective.

"Are you planning to toss out another accusation, Detective? It better be a good one because I am not going to go back to the station to answer any more questions, and neither is anyone else, not without a lawyer present. So, unless you've got a good reason to harass us, I suggest you wrap things up as quickly as possible. Is there anything else we can help you with?"

The detective met Steve's stare and shook his head slowly. He glanced fleetingly at James and Bruno before settling on Maxine.

"No, I'm done here for now. I apologize if I've overstepped my bounds."

He shuffled and picked up his computer, taking his time turning it off, casually standing as we waited. He settled his dark eyes on me.

"I would caution everyone to be careful. Your neighbor will likely be released before the end of the night, and there appears to be a little tension between the two families. He'll be warned to steer clear of your property, and I suggest resisting the urge to engage him in conversation. If it wasn't clear a moment ago, I need to inform you that our investigation has now changed."

James was blinking. "What do you mean? How has it changed?"

"Both Aster and Alex's deaths are officially considered suspicious death investigations, not accidents. I suggest everyone stay reachable for the next few days."

After the detective left, we moved into the kitchen for hot tea. Maxine put her old whistle kettle on the burner to boil water, and I rummaged around and found mugs. Maxine pulled out her collection of leaves, spices, and natural sweeteners and insisted we try her special homemade blend. James and Bruno watched from the counter. Steve hovered close behind me. Maxine announced her plan to crush the leaves in a mortar and use mesh tea balls. She loved to mix and match the herbs and chatted to a silent James and Bruno as if a policeman had not just announced they believed a murderer was on the loose. I didn't want to leave the kitchen, but Steve pulled me into the next room with a firm hand, muttering that we needed to talk.

He did not let go of my hand but pulled it up to his face to look at the ring. He grinned happily at me.

"It isn't what you think it means," I said.

"You're wearing it," he said. "What else could it mean?"

"I didn't want to lose it."

I took my hand back and twisted the ring loose, but didn't take it all the way off, wondering what to do. I didn't want to give it back to him, and I didn't want him to think we were back together. In the back of my mind, something told me that it probably wasn't a good idea to admit I might give the ring to Bruno. After seeing him stare down that detective, I had a healthy respect for him and thought he would not like that plan. His little display of male dominance had been impressive, but it was also a bit intimidating.

"Okay then, give it back," he teased.

"No." I pushed it back on.

He chuckled at me, and I eyed him.

"Did you really design this ring? Did you really see it in a dream? Tell me the truth, Steve. You made up that story, didn't you?"

His grin has always been one of his finer points, and at that moment, he was at one hundred percent charm.`

"It's the honest truth," he said. "Your beautiful eyes enslaved me from the start."

I stepped away from him because my emotions were waffling again. *Too freaking easy.*

"Don't you think the stone is exactly like that drawing on the bottle of wine Bruno brought?"

His eyes narrowed, and his smile disappeared. He crossed his arms over his chest looking dangerous.

"What are you saying?" Steve asked. "What did that little devil tell you?"

I held the ring up, the diamonds sparkled in the light.

"Bruno claims that this is a family heirloom, and it was sent to Maxine years ago. Is that the real truth? Please, just tell me the real truth."

He stared at the ring, then stared at me.

"What do you have to say about that, Steve? It's the same type of stone on the label of his bottle from Brazil. That's too much of a coincidence, don't you think? That this ring and that bottle of wine bear the same type of stone, a stone that comes from his family mine in Brazil. Don't you agree that it's quite a coincidence?"

Steve tightened his lips, disappointed with me. He shut his eyes for several long seconds, then opened them again, staring right at me.

"Last year, when my uncle contacted Maxine for money, he attempted to entice her with gemstones from Brazil. Maxine wouldn't have anything to do with him, but he was my uncle, so I sent him money and told him to send a few gemstones in return. That's how I obtained the center blue stone in your ring," he growled. "Then, you came along, and your lovely eyes matched that stone perfectly."

Steve slammed a closed fist on the side table.

"And then we fell in love, and I had that beautiful dream about your eyes that the gemstone matched perfectly, commissioned that ring, asked you to marry me, and we were happy. We were *happy*."

"Steve, I—"

"I'm going to kill him." His face had completely tensed. He frightened me.

"Wait, no."

My mind was in a complete tailspin. Was Steve telling the truth? He looked so earnest, wounded. Could Bruno have been lying? *Gad!*

If Bruno lied, then why did he return the ring? I was beyond confused, and my head began to pound painfully. Then, an overwhelming fear set in. If what the detective said was true, if the deaths of Alex and Aster were not accidents, if they were murdered, then who was to blame?

Bruno? James? Chucky? Steve? Maxine?

Certainly not Maxine or Steve, I spent enough time with them to know they were not capable of murder. And Chucky seemed unlikely too. Why would he suddenly start killing his neighbors, especially when he was sleeping with Aster? That left James and Bruno, two men I did not know very well, and of the two of them, Bruno was the biggest outsider.

No, not Bruno, I silently shouted back. He was too wounded and tried to warn me away. He hadn't even met Alex. He wanted to stay at a hotel. And our afternoon in the bungalow, he couldn't be that good an actor. His energy did not emit violence in the least! *Am I being an absolute idiot, just because the scent of him stirred me up?*

Maybe it was James.

I stared at Steve, the man I had known for months, my familiar, and I reached out and grasped his wrist.

"Please don't go in there and fight anybody," I said softly.

"So, you believe that stranger over me?" Steve's voice faded out.

"No," I said. "I don't know what to believe."

"This is bullshit, Amanda. Don't you get it? He spun up a fairy tale to ensure that you stay angry at me. Don't fall for it. He needs to secure his cut of the trust. If we marry, and if by some miracle we get pregnant, the trust will fall completely to us. He can't allow that to happen."

I hit him in the chest with both fists.

"Dammit, Steve, this is why it's so hard for me to believe you. I asked you about this! The heir clause in that trust. The other day, I asked you point blank, and you lied to me. Ever since that stupid box in the closet you've been lying to me on a daily basis. How am I supposed to believe anything you say if you keep lying to me?"

I'd never seen Steve cry, but his eyes were blinking away. His lips trembled, and his face and neck turned pink. Tears pooled in the corner of each of his eyes.

"I'm sorry." A single tear rolled down his cheek. "I did lie to you. I lied about all of it, everything." He sobbed, and it was crazy upsetting to see a big man sob. His entire body shook with it. "After what you told me, about your professor, I hid everything. I didn't want you to see it or discover some of the things I've done. I'm a terrible person, Amanda. I don't deserve you."

That's how I found myself hugging and consoling him. *I was too easy!* Here he was, confessing that I had been right all along, and I was consoling him for being a liar! He got himself back under control and searched me with those puppy eyes.

"And the heir clause, I didn't divulge anything about it because I didn't want you to assume my proposal had anything to do with the money in that trust. You were already furious at me, and I feared losing you. I panicked. I wish that clause and that trust didn't exist." A few more tears rolled down his cheeks. "I'm sorry." One last emotional sob escaped his chest.

"Oh, Steve."

I wiped away his tears and pulled him into another hug. Somewhere in the back of my mind, a voice told me to just admit that I was going to marry him and be done with it. Why else would I want to believe him so badly? And my fixation with Bruno was probably an illusion because Bruno resembled Steve. Those thoughts deflated me. After a moment, I loosened my grip, and we separated a bit. I gave him a small peck on the lips. I don't know why, call it a habit. He wore a hopeful expression.

"That doesn't mean we're back together," I said. "And it doesn't mean I've decided what to believe. Let's just say, I don't completely not believe all of your bullshit. Not yet."

He dipped his head.

"Now, we should go in there and drink some tea."

He nodded.

"But promise to play nice."

He bobbed his head.

Chapter 14

They made three varieties of tea. James had insisted on teaching Maxine a way to sweeten the tea with licorice and candy leaf, something he carried everywhere, and Bruno had suggested they each make a version of tea for everyone to try. Bruno had brought tea and coffee, along with the wine from Brazil, and had been waiting for the right moment to share it. Maxine said we were going to have a blind taste test and vote on which tea everyone found the tastiest.

As we gathered around the kitchen island, James creased his brow and pressed his lips together when he spotted the engagement ring still on my finger. Had he expected me to return it to Steve?

"Everyone has three cups," Maxine pointed to the cups, each filled with different varieties of tea.

"We need to give each tea a fair chance," Bruno said. "To cleanse the palette and experience the flavors, we should drink at least half of each sample. The subtle flavors in our Brazilian teas are delicate, and you need to give your taste buds a chance to acclimate to them." He picked up a smaller cup, which was probably his family tea, and smiled.

I turned my face away, disappointed in my own wavering loyalties. Perhaps Bruno and Steve were more alike than I thought. Perhaps they were both easy liars and classic manipulators. Perhaps neither was honest. The thought choked my heart.

"I'm going to come out and say something," James announced. "I've decided to file a petition against Grandpa's wording of the trust. I'm calling it illegal and unethical and unfair."

Everyone stared at him as we sipped our teas.

"Mr. Daxter already told us your plan." Maxine smiled at him. "But I'm afraid you'll not get far with your motions. I never did."

"Some of it contains hate language," James continued, glancing at my ring, then at Steve. "That might make a difference in today's court. And it's only fair that the trust is split fifty-fifty, between his two sons or their legitimate offspring, regardless of who marries who. We've already discussed it, right, Steve? A fifty-fifty split is fair. You said you wouldn't contest my motion."

James completed his tea in one gulp and picked up the next cup. He turned to Maxine.

"I'm not sure if I should drink everything, did anyone add sugar? I already kind of overdid it at Swabbies."

"Oh, James," Maxine patted his hand. "Live a little. That's what your insulin is for. Regardless, I only added a smidge of sugar to my own cup, for taste. You should be fine."

"I added no sweetener," Bruno assured him. "But sometimes a little honey is nice."

James turned back to Steve. "Are you still in agreement with me about the trust?"

Steve glanced at me briefly.

"Of course, James. But what about Bruno here? If we don't contest all of the wording, it can be a three-way split. With your motion, you'd have to chop Uncle Rick's half between the two of you. I'm okay with one-third, like Maxine said, that's probably what's going to happen anyway. Maybe we can think of a way to keep the company intact by buying each other out. We'll work it out later. And don't worry about that stupid clause. Although we love each other, Amanda might need a little more time before tying the knot."

"You are forgetting that my father leaves a widow," Bruno said simply.

"He was disinherited before that marriage." James glared at Bruno. "In fact, he was disinherited before you were born. The way my motion is going to read, anything he did after abandoning this family doesn't count. I'm sorry, Bruno, but he left us years ago without looking back. We won't leave you totally out to dry. I'd be willing to invest in your winery after the trust is dispersed correctly."

"It's not going to fly in court," Steve said, but everyone could see the glimmer in his eye.

Bruno fixed his jaw. "You propose robbing a widow."

"Boys! Let's not talk about this anymore. Let's just try to forget all this nonsense."

Maxine rested her hand on James's and ferried over a pink box with the words "mochi dough" stencil in gold on top. It had been sitting on the kitchen island.

"I was saving them for tomorrow morning, but why don't we have them now?" She opened the box to reveal donuts. "Don't they look exactly like baby teething rings? Now, James, don't be a party pooper. The purple ones are sugar-free. Go on, I insist. We need some sweetness right now. You handsome boys are my favorite men in the world, and I'd like you all to be pleasant to each other, even if for only a few minutes. We need a few positive moments, to remember we are all family."

"Where'd you get these?" Steve dove right into the doughnuts.

"Kira took me to a place on the way home," Maxine said. "Over by the bookstore. Her kids love the bubble tea there. Goodness, the tea she buys, the prices! But they sell these perfectly cute donuts, and I couldn't resist."

I chuckled. "Milk tea with boba?"

She winked at me, then Maxine set out small plates and forks for a full-on tea party. No one was getting away with skipping the tea or tasting the treats. She actually tutted at James until he took a bite of one of the purple donuts. His face broke into a small smile.

"Sugar-free," she assured him, nibbling on a purple one herself. "So, don't be shy with it. Isn't this just what we need? A cozy little tea party to put things into perspective. We've had too much bad news around here, too much sadness and anxious feelings. I don't want to hear anymore bickering or talking about trust funds. Now drink your tea, kids, and we'll have that vote."

The donuts tasted sweet and were melt-in-your-mouth satisfying. I watched James eat his treat suspiciously, but he finished the entire pastry and licked his fingers. Maxine pointed out a spare purple sugar-free treat in the box, but he shook his head. She poured us all more of the mug of tea because we had already finished all the liquid in our cups. Hands down, the mug tea got our votes, Maxine's special blend. We sat quietly, and I began to feel tired and emotionally drained.

"I better go check my sugar." James stood and walked slowly toward his room. He paused at the refrigerator to retrieve his little vial of insulin.

"Do you want your pen back?" Maxine asked him. "The doctor gave me a new one."

"No, no. You've already used it." James smiled at her. "I got it with this."

We watched him meander slowly out of the room.

"I feel strange." Bruno's eyes were alert as he stood, and those worried eyes zeroed in on me. "Do you feel strange?"

But Maxine chimed in instead.

"Oh, I feel wiped out. That was a tough day, but a very nice little tea party. But now I'm sleepy," she said. "I bet we're all tuckered out. We should all retire."

Steve yawned at me. "I'll walk you to your door?"

"Amanda?" Bruno still stared at me.

"She's tired," Steve said to him firmly. "I'm walking the girls to their rooms, and you should back off." Steve put his hands on his hips and stared menacingly at Bruno. "I know what happened, everything, and I'll deal with you later."

Perhaps it was that sugar-filled donut, but I felt a deep sleep calling me and nodded at Steve. I ignored Bruno's staring eyes when I said goodnight. I did not want to look at him and have to decide if he was the untruthful one or not. It was extremely late, and I was extremely tired. I wanted to believe in Bruno, but I wanted to believe in Steve too, and I couldn't believe them both. Somebody was lying, and I had no idea who.

"I'm okay," I said in his general direction. "Let's just all go to sleep."

Steve and I headed down the back hall with Maxine. At her door, we paused to give goodnight hugs, like we'd done a million times before. It felt normal, familiar, comforting. Maxine bent forward to whisper in my ear.

"I'm glad to see this back on your finger." She clutched my hand.

I felt guilty, but also pleased. Maxine was happy with me. Steve was happy with me. Was I happy with myself? I did the reasoning in my head, I did not know Bruno, not really, but I did know Steve. We had been blissfully happy for months. Happy and in love and set to start a wonderful life together. *We could have babies.* Was I ready to throw it all away? I wasn't sure.

I adored that big house, and Maxine had insisted we live in it after we married, to raise our family. She had been the mother, the sister, the best friend I never had, and she couldn't wait for her first great-grandchild. Around Maxine and Steve, I always felt adored and loved, part of a clan. I had to admit, I wanted that feeling back again.

Steve opened the door for me. He waited as I passed into my bedroom and turned. He stood just outside, looking sleepy and handsome. A sudden flood of nostalgia hit me.

Was there a way to get it all back, the life we had last month?

Did I really want it back? *Yes!* I was already thirty-three years old and had never worked a regular job in my life. My entire world had been freelance writing, gig after gig, unstable, insecure, and nomadic. My life at the river mansion had been stable, and I could become a mother with Steve, I could see it. *If I could only trust him.* Perhaps we had hit a turning point earlier, with those tears he shed, when he had finally admitted his lies. Perhaps it was possible to love him again. I could certainly see a life with Steve. The days, the kids, the holidays were all crystal clear in my mind. I could see a future with him, if I could just trust him again.

And I couldn't see any future from believing Bruno, even though his dark eyes, hair, and skin infiltrated my thoughts. I willed myself to block out his insidious image. I just wanted my happy future again.

"Steve?"

That's all I needed to say. I was suddenly in his warm arms, and his mouth claimed mine in a familiar kiss. He ran his hands over my back and muttered in my ear. He left a trail of tender kisses along my neck, but it wasn't the same. It was nowhere near what had been there before. It was nowhere near what had happened the other afternoon with Bruno. I became extremely upset, realizing I had lost everything after all, and began to cry.

"Don't cry," he whispered. "It's okay. We're going to be okay. I'm sorry about all of it, Amanda, and you'll see, everything will be fine."

He hugged me again, holding me tight, securing me in his arms. I let out a long sigh, finally relaxing. Maybe, with just a little more time, we could get it all back. I let my hands go around his neck and returned his embrace. Somehow, he had kicked the door closed behind us and maneuvered us to the bed. He kissed me sloppily one, twice. We dropped to sit on the bed, and he cupped my face in his hands, familiar, easy.

I felt so groggy. He was talking again.

"We can do this. We can get through this together. That's what I think, what about you? What do you think?" His voice came out in a mumbled mess.

"I wish I could go back and do a few things differently."

"Me too, me too," he chuckled, "God, I keep thinking, why didn't I toss that stupid box into the dumpster? Why didn't I just get rid of it? We could have avoided all of this."

He must have seen my face and felt me stiffen. *Gad, that box!* I dragged myself away from him. *I was too easy!* Why were my limbs so heavy? I was aware that I was about to fall asleep. My eyes could barely stay open.

"No…" I managed, then passed out.

Chapter 15

A base drum pulsed in my head, and that beat was accompanied with a dry mouth, blurry vision, heavy limbs, and a mega headache. Someone stepped heavily in my bungalow, and the walls appear to tilt. I pushed delicately into a sitting position, but moved too fast, and the blood drained from my head, causing me to feel nauseous. It took a concerted effort to crack my eyelids enough to see a tall man coming into the bedroom with a large glass of water. Steve sank heavily on the mattress and delivered the water.

"Thank you." My voice sounded like a dying frog.

I greedily gulped the entire glass. Steve took the glass and attempted to shake out the last little drops for himself. I cleared my throat.

"I feel terrible."

"Me too," he said. "It's four o'clock in the afternoon."

No way! I stared at him, but he wasn't kidding.

"We were drugged," he said. "You went out like a light, and I couldn't stay awake enough to even stand up. I already downed two glasses of water, but I'm still thirsty."

He helped me rise out of the bed. I never felt so unglamorous, still wearing my wrinkled dress from the previous night.

"How long have you been awake?"

"Long enough to drink the two glasses of water," he said.

I carefully made my way to the kitchen, holding onto the walls for support. Two glasses of water sounded good.

"Maybe it was something in the tea," he said.

"The tea?"

"What else could it have been?"

"Oh goodness, we should check on Maxine!" My chest constricted.

His face broke into a panic. He started moving too fast for me to track.

"I'll go right now."

He scrambled back to the bedroom, and I heard him burst out the door. After finishing another full glass of water, I dragged myself to the bathroom to get cleaned up. I splashed cold water on my face and tried to tame my unruly blonde hair. A quick ponytail would have to do, and a quick brush of the teeth. I was eager to go see how that old woman was doing. *Could Maxine survive being drugged like that?* My chest flooded with dread. *No, no, don't panic,* I told myself. Just as I emerged from the small bathroom, Steve pushed the outside door open and reentered the room. He shrugged nonchalantly at me.

"Maxine is fine, she's watching her standard TV program."

"Oh, thank goodness." My entire body relaxed.

"She said she felt funny last night, vomited, then went to sleep. She woke up fine, a little groggy and thirsty, but fine."

"She vomited?" I asked.

"Yeah, she's been up for hours. She says everyone's been sleeping. She thought maybe James and Bruno tied one on and were sleeping it off, and that we were cooped up making… well, that we were over here making up." He reached out to touch my shoulder.

"No."

He pursed his lips,

"If we break up," he said, "she'll… It'll break her."

I turned away from him, embarrassed about those late-night kisses. My head was still pounding, and my heart was now cracking. We very nearly got back together, but we were not on the same page about what went wrong. Heat rose up my neck. Steve was *not* honest. What did that make Bruno? Bruno.

"Bruno felt funny too," I recalled softly. "So, maybe the tea had been tainted. Could it have been on purpose? Who would do such a thing? Could it have been James and his herbal sticks? You say Maxine hasn't seen them? We need to check on them."

Steve wore a sour expression. "Why are you so concerned about Bruno?" he asked.

"Something feels wrong. That detective basically told us that someone put those pills in Aster's tin. Do you think James did it? He's been so angry and focused on that trust fund. Bruno was suspicious of him last night at dinner, and he was actually a little scared. Do you have any idea why James would drug everyone?"

Steve blinked. "Let's go ask him."

We walked purposely into the house, and I felt dread. What would we find? I could hear Maxine in the den watching an afternoon game show. We turned toward the far bedrooms where James and Bruno were staying on opposite sides of the hallway. My heart clattered out of control.

What if something happened to Bruno? I would never forgive myself for minimizing his fears and walking away the previous night, for behaving as if he were the dishonest one.

"James?" Steve knocked on James's door and waited.

"Bruno?" I knocked on Bruno's door. Nobody answered.

We both knocked again.

"James?" Steve repeated.

"Bruno?" I said again.

No answers. Why didn't they answer? Steve gave me a raised brow.

Steve slowly opened James's door while I slowly opened Bruno's, all the while my anxiety shook off the charts as my hand wavered on the door knob. Hopefully, I was only invading his privacy, disturbing his sleep. Hopefully, I'd only find him upset at me for not believing in him, allowing Steve to walk me to my door, for leading him on in several different ways, and then running directly back to my fiancé.

The door swung open, and I peeked into the room. No one was there. I moved inside and glanced around. The small bathroom was empty, the bed was pristine, and his backpack was on a chair in the corner. I backed up, out of the room, and closed the door just as Steve gasped loudly.

James lay across his bed still wearing clothes from the previous night. His color was light, his mouth was open, and he appeared dead. Steve flipped him to his back and searched his neck for a pulse. His frantic eyes search me out.

"He's so cold," Steve said. "And I can't find a pulse, call 911."

The ambulance sped off just as Detective Allen arrived in his vintage mustang. Although we couldn't find a pulse, the medic assured us that James wasn't dead, only in a coma, likely due to his sugar level. He had injected himself with something, and we found a needle next to the small insulin container. Everything had been laying on his bedsheets next to him.

The detective jumped out of his car and walked directly toward the three of us, Steve, Maxine, and myself.

"Another tragic accident?" He watched the ambulance speed away. He turned back to us. "There seems to be someone missing."

"It's Bruno, we can't find him," I said rapidly. "We think something may have happened to him."

The detective narrowed his eyes. "Have you checked the entire house? Can you tell me how long he has been missing?"

"We checked everywhere, but he's not here." Maxine turned her back on the detective and went into the house. She looked exhausted. Poor Maxine.

"He's not here, he isn't anywhere," Steve echoed Maxine.

"How long has he been missing? He was here last night at our meeting, looking fine. Was he around this morning?"

Both Steve and I exchanged glances.

"He retired about the same time we did last night," Steve said. "That's the last we saw of him. I will say, his bed doesn't look slept in."

"He was feeling funny last night, we were all feeling funny, like maybe we ate or drank something bad," I said rapidly. My voice had gone high and hysterical. "All of his stuff is still in the house, so he didn't leave. He's got to be around here somewhere! I think we were drugged. We had been knocked out for hours!"

Steve and the detective stared at me, then Steve started toward the house.

"I need to check on Maxine."

The detective considered me. "Drugged? Tell me more about that."

The detective had a couple of uniformed police officers search the grounds. They spent a few hours looking over the levy edge and visited each of the neighboring homes. Chucky had returned the previous night, so they spend a good amount of time talking to him. I painstakingly searched every nook in the house, every closet and every corner, even the pool storage room Maxine kept locked. Steve followed me for some of my search but gave up after I started rechecking places. He ended up on the back patio sitting with the detective and sharing a pitcher of tea. They were quietly reviewing the information the detective had on that computer pad. Steve stood up, kissed me on the cheek, and held a chair for me. He poured another glass of tea and gave it to me.

"He's gone." I was worried. "It's like he fell off the face of the earth."

The two men exchanged glances.

"Something knocked us all out last night," I said. "Did Steve mention that he also believes someone tainted the tea? It's not just me. I don't know how that could happen, unless it was James, Bruno, or Maxine, but that seems ludicrous, why drug yourself? Maybe Chucky snuck over and added something to Maxine's tea tin? Has he been questioned about it?"

The detective quietly listened. Had they already considered that?

"What if Bruno wandered off and fell into a crevice or something? What if he fell into the water?"

Steve shook his head. "I don't think he fell in the water."

"How do you know?" I demanded. "Someone needs to search the river. He could be stuck somewhere downstream. Isn't there a search and rescue we can call? Last night, I passed out quite suddenly, it was sudden. I couldn't keep my eyes open, remember? What if something similar happened to him."

The detective leaned back with his hands on his chin. His eyes darted from me to Steve and back again. He leaned forward.

"A preliminary report came in a little earlier, and I just relayed the message to Mr. Winters here." His overly bushy brows arched over his eyes. "It appears that James Winters injected himself with the same beta-blocking medication that we found in Aster's tin of pills. His vial of insulin was full of it, so it wasn't an accident."

That information turned my body to lead. *Not an accident.* Definitely not an accident. My chest compressed into a suffocating feeling on that beautiful open, fresh air patio.

"What do you both know about Bruno?" he asked. "How long have you known him?"

"We've only just met him," Steve said. "Even last year, when my uncle contacted us, he was only mentioned by name. Our first direct contact with Bruno was a little over a week ago. The first time any of us ever spoke directly to him was when he called to tell us my uncle had passed."

The detective nodded, scrolling through the document on his computer pad.

"It's clear that he's after money," Steve kept talking, "specifically, money from the trust my grandfather set up. It's due to be liquidated in six months, and he's determined to get a piece of that pie. He brought questionable paperwork from Brazil and claims a vested interest. He has even…" Steve avoided looking directly at me. "He's even tried to seduce my fiancé in an effort to stir us up. He's tried to stir the pot in several ways, like subtle jabs to get James riled and telling fabricated tales to Amanda, and now that I think about it, he might have pushed Alex over the side of that riverbank wall."

"That seems farfetched," I spat out. "Bruno hadn't even arrived until late the night Alex slipped. He had no idea who Alex was, they never even met."

"You mean, as far as we know he arrived late at night." Steve's eyes were hard. "Have you ever wondered why it took Bruno so long to get to the house? His plane landed at Sacramento International before seven in the evening, and he didn't show up at the front door until well after midnight. This house is less than 5 miles away from the airport, Amanda, so why did it take him so long to get here?"

"Why do you think it took him so long?" My voice sounded exasperated.

"I don't think it took him long at all. I think he was spying on us," Steve said. "I think he spent the time spying on us. Casing the place, finding out our weaknesses, formulating his plan, figuring out how to pit us all against one another, and then…"

I stood up. My eyes volleyed between Steve and the detective. Did the detective take Steve seriously? Yes, of course, he did. He diligently jotted everything into his computer pad.

"You actually believe Bruno came here to kill off everyone in your family and steal your trust fund?"

Steve also stood. "It makes the most sense. All of this started happening when Bruno arrived, and if he's so innocent, where is he?"

Yes, where was Bruno? My heart pounded in my chest.

"Everyone was drugged last night, Bruno included. He felt funny, remember? He probably washed downstream, and no one seems to care."

"Anyone can say they feel funny," Steve snapped. "But the truth is, nobody saw him pass out. We didn't see him after we went to the guest house."

"Guess what? I didn't see you pass out, either," I said.

Red fury radiated from Steve's face. The detective started to stand as Steve shouted at me.

"Why are you defending him so strongly? Did you *fuck* him?" He pointed his finger at me. "You did, didn't you? You actually fucked him, didn't you?"

"No! That's not what happened. We only—"

"I knew it!" Steve shouted. "The afternoon with the t-shirt, your face, I didn't want to believe it, but I knew it! You said you only kissed him, but you actually fucked that little fucker!"

Then, for one brief moment, a quiet, heated minute passed in which everyone held their breath.

Out on the manicured lawn, one of the uniformed policemen had stopped to stare. All I wanted was to melt into the recently sanded and refinished redwood slats. I finally let my breath out, not able to meet anyone's eye.

"You barely know him, Amanda," he said. "I can't believe you did this to us."

"How dare you," I sputtered. "I am not going to stand here and listen to this. I'm going to go back to my room."

Steve bellowed, *"Fuck!"* which made me jump as it reverberated and filled the entire five acres of Maxine's lawn.

"Mr. Winters," the detective's voice trailed and faded. "You'll need to calm down and…"

I couldn't help glancing over my shoulder. In the center of the lawn, both the uniformed policeman and that little devil watched me greedily.

You are freaking too easy, the devil blinked before disappearing into her hidey-hole.

How dare she judge me! I did not *fuck* Bruno! We only slept together! As in *sleep*. There may have been a little fooling around, and a missing bikini top, but that was it. We did not do *that*. Yet, the guilt slowly filled into every little pore in my skin.

Chapter 16

After a few hours, the police departed. I watched the detective's cool convertible drive off tailing a squad car. The flood lights blared to life in the backyard. Every porch light burned, and the party lights blazed. Maxine's voice carried shrilly, and Steve yelled in return. They were bickering. Though I couldn't quite hear everything, they were quarreling about me. It was a heated argument that ended with a slamming door.

Soon, I felt the bungalow shake. Someone was on the plank walkway stomping toward my back door. The bedroom door rattled loudly, and Steve burst into the den. I sprang to a stand.

"How dare you!" I said. "You cannot just barge in here."

He scowled at me, face red with rage. He pointed a finger. "You! You're trying to make me out to be the bad one! You're shouting at me?"

Good lord, he was angry! I scrambled behind the thick easy chair. He hit the wall with his fist and pointed toward the big house.

"She expects me to apologize to you, to *you*!" he growled. "Do you know what you did to her? What she's going through? She's a fragile old woman!"

He was ranting. His bulging eyes moved everywhere. He looked ready to pounce.

"I... I...I..." I couldn't think of a thing to say.

"I finally told her. I had no choice but to tell her what you did with him, that you..." he physically choked on the words. His eyes cringed in agony. He took three deep breaths. "Now she's crying. And she blames me for what you did, if that isn't a slap in the fucking face! I'm the bad guy."

He started yelling again, pacing, looking ready to strangle something—like my neck. His eyes shot daggers at me.

"She wants me to forgive you and get over it. I'm supposed to fix all of this, but to tell the truth, I'm not sure if I want to fix anything anymore. I will not accept a wife, or a fiancé, or a woman who could easily betray me like you did, and right under my nose. Good God, woman, do you have no shame? He's ten years younger than you!"

"Do I have no shame?" He was unbelievable. "You're the one who participated in questionable sexual behavior with his students and even video-taped it. Do any of those girls know you filmed it? The things you did with them? I counted twelve thumb drives in that box, all dated this past term, Steve. All while you were supposedly falling in love with me! If you're trying to convince me you're a faithful man, go back and look at the evidence in your closet."

He pointed a finger at me. "I stopped all of that after we got engaged. That's why everything was packed in a box in the closet! I never cheated on you after we got engaged, not once. I have been an honorable and faithful fiancé to you! You can't say the same to me."

"We were only engaged for two weeks! And technically, I never cheated on you, either. We were broken up when things happened with Bruno, and you know what, we are still broken up, and we're going to stay broken up."

"I'm going to leave because right now I feel like snapping your neck," he hissed.

A cold chill ran down my spine. I've heard him speak harshly before, but never toward me. *Is he capable of snapping a neck?*

Echoes of Steve's most recent threats flooded my brain. Words he said to other people, and those people were gone. To Alex, *I'm going to kill you*, and the next day Alex was dead. When Aster stomped away from him the other night, he had mumbled something about *shutting her up for good,* and soon after that, Aster was dead, never to talk again. Finally, the previous night, he stared Bruno down and snarled, *I'll deal with you later,* and since that statement, Bruno has been missing.

So, it was a valid question: was Steve capable of snapping a neck? My neck? Was it possible to be so completely wrong about a person after months of intimate interactions?

"You'd better lock your door tonight," he growled.

"Am I in danger?" It came out in a near whisper. "Is that a threat?"

His eyes closed, and his face drooped. He hit the wall again, adding more than a dent. This time, he left a proper hole.

"Dammit, Amanda!" he hissed. "I don't know who's in danger, but your *boyfriend* is out there, probably casing the place. I'm going to leave all the lights on and turn on the security system, but you should lock the doors too. I'm going to sleep in the main house because Maxine is scared to death. I don't think he's after you, so you're probably safe. I think it's me he's after, anyone who stands in the way of that trust fund."

I opened my mouth, but nothing came out.

"Even though I'd like to wring your neck, you are not in danger from me." His puppy dog eyes were so sad. "I can't even believe you could think that."

He turned and walked away from me, reminding me to lock the door as he slammed it shut.

I cried. What else could I do? I cried and cried. My thoughts drifted back to the day Maxine and I met, at the Bay Area Book Festival. We both sat front and center in a crowd listening to the author of one of my ghostwriting gigs take questions about his latest best seller. All the women in the audience gushed about how he depicted the feminine voice, impressed with his grasp of how women thought. I never met the author in person, all our correspondence had been via computer, so he had no idea I was there. It didn't bother me when he took credit for quotable phrases the audience praised, I just reveled in the fact that people were inspired with my writing. The positive accolades he received gave me hope. If I ever finished my thriller, maybe it would be a success.

Maxine twiddled next to me and tutted. I glanced at her.

"Listen to that windbag," she whispered. "There isn't a way in hell that man wrote that book."

I chuckled at her. She leaned toward me.

"He used a ghostwriter," she nodded at me. "I'd put money on it. Everyone is doing it nowadays."

She was right, of course, but I just grinned at her.

We spent the day strolling through the vendors, exclaiming over books we'd both read and raved about. We shared tidbits of our lives, astounded to learn we attended the same primary school and grew up in the same town, practically neighbors, but in different decades. When I finally confessed that I was indeed a ghostwriter and had contributed a fair amount of material to the author we had been listening to, Maxine insisted I ghostwrite for her. She was having trouble with the beginning section of her memoir, the early years, she said. Since I was familiar with the places she needed to describe, she made me an offer I couldn't refuse: room and board in a riverfront cottage with free utilities and fifty thousand dollars at the end of the year. All for ghostwriting, with the goal to complete three chapters, the *Part One* of her memoir. How could anyone say no to such an offer?

Steve visited the day I moved into the cottage and then regularly dropped in every other night that first month. He was entertaining and handsome, but I kept him at a distance in the beginning, because I had vowed to steer clear of men I found attractive. I didn't trust my radar when it came to them and had resolved to never fall in love. But eventually, I lingered at the main house longer and longer when he dropped in to see Maxine, anticipating his visits and the mini-adventures he ferried us to. Maxine adored him, so I thought he must be a fantastic human.

It was the stories from Maxine that really cemented my interest. He had been orphaned at six, after a car accident took his parents. An aunt that was raising him committed suicide a year later. Because she had cancer, Maxine stated.

His grandfather had been hard on him, driving him to succeed, but Steve was a poet at heart. He was sensitive and caring and had built up a wall of male charisma to hide it. I watched him dote on Maxine, bringing her flowers and sugar-free pastries from the Freemont Bakery. Once a week, he took her to a fancy dinner and treated her like a queen. He enjoyed romance movies, and I found that irresistibly attractive. He had read all the classics, even the Bronte sisters, and loved a good book discussion. He became the inspiration for my male main character, the love interest in my thriller, after our first kiss. I had been completely smitten with him.

It became *love* when he spontaneously lauded an excerpt I wrote for Maxine. He casually admired my use of semi-colons and imagery one evening. He had stared right into my eyes and told me the one thing I'd always longed to hear: that I should write my own novels. *The world needs to hear your voice.* That was his advice as a creative writing teacher. He was mesmerized by me, he said, by my brain, my humor, and finally, by my body. I no longer felt invisible.

Soon after our physical relationship took off, he began treating me like a queen, offering the same consideration and respect as his grandmother, and it miraculously became possible to have it all; writing for myself, having a home, a financially stable life, a husband, and maybe even children. Steve made me feel like my life wasn't completely ruined after all.

But it was all lost now, to oblivion, and I cried. I cried for losing what could have been. Perhaps, my only shot at a future family. My destiny pointed toward a lonely nomadic existence again, ghostwriting for pennies while hoping to be taken seriously. How had it all gone so wrong so quickly?

In my self-pity, I stared out at the back lawn, all ablaze like a carnival ride. The devil in the oak was probably hiding in that dark hole, and I wondered where Bruno could be. Did I believe he was a dangerous man? No. Yes. Not really. Maybe. Everything in my system shouted that Bruno was the guy I should trust, but my system had been wrong too many times before. My system was as untrustworthy as all the men around me.

My mind suddenly drifted to James. How was he, and who had tainted his insulin? During our heated argument, we hadn't even thought to mention him. Steve hadn't been concerned about James in the least. Then, I recalled how James, Bruno, and I had gathered up Maxine's pills the day she spilled them. I remember watching Bruno slowly add pills into a clear baggy. Is that when he got a hold of them? *No, Bruno was not the bad guy!* I patted my swollen eyes, poured a glass of water, and went to bed.

Chapter 17

An odd sound jolted me out of sleep. Or was it the shuddering of the bungalow? Those vibration always happened when someone climbed the outer steps to the front door or walked the planks from the main house. It was my silent alert that a visitor approached. I sat up in bed and closed my eyes, attempting to sense if someone was out there, but nothing was shaking now. If someone lurked outside, they had stopped moving.

Very slowly, I slipped out of my bed and took the gentlest steps to the half wall that separated the den from the bedroom. I stared into the darkness, searching for any sign of movement. Nothing. It was pitch black outside the sliding glass door. That seemed odd. The digital clock on my nightstand was blank.

The electricity was out, which explained the dark night. All those lights Steve lit were out, which meant the electricity was out at the big house too. Only the tinkle of the river made a sound, and I began to feel insecure. I took a few tentative steps toward the patio but froze when I heard the gentle rap.

Tap, tap, tap.

Someone tapped on the back glass window to my bedroom door, the door that opened to the plank connection to the big house. The window appeared dark, and no one peeked in. My pulse began to pick up. If Steve was out there, he'd be peeking in. I searched for something to use as a weapon, then stepped over to my nightstand to retrieve my cell phone. It had been on the charger and had charged to seventy percent before the electricity had gone out. It was two thirty-three in the morning. Nothing in my bedroom could pass for a proper weapon, and I almost dialed 911, but the tapping resumed, startling me. A small hand materialized in the window, wearing familiar leather gloves. Maxine.

I glided quickly to the door and stood on tiptoes to look out the small window. Yes, it was Maxine! Relief escaped my chest in a sigh. I quickly unlocked the door and let her in. She urged me to shut the door behind her. She wore a long robe tied snuggly at the waist. She glanced at the phone in my hand.

"Did you call someone?" she asked.

"No," I said. "Should I? What's going on? Is the electricity out?"

She nodded. "Everything's out." She moved her head to peer into the den, then clutched my arm with her gloved hand. "There is an emergency battery in the back bedroom. It opens a door in cases like this. I've never told you before, but there's a panic room in the house. Just a little closet of a room, but big enough for the two of us."

"Oh, God, I should call someone. Where's Steve?"

She patted my hand, calming me. "I've already called, and they're on the way. I don't know where Steve is."

"Is someone out there? Is something wrong?"

"I don't know, but better safe than sorry. I came to get you, just in case. We can hide in the panic closet until the police get here." She smiled at me.

I nodded and pulled on a pair of shorts and a hoodie over my thin shirt. When I looked back at her, I got the surprise of my life. Maxine had a gun. She held it out to me with a shaking hand.

"Take it," she urged. "I don't think I'll be able to operate it."

"A gun? Maxine!"

"Steve insisted I keep it in my bedside table. But heavens, I'm an old lady. I wouldn't have the strength to fire it, let alone hold it steady. It weighs a ton. Take it, Amanda, you'd better be in charge of it. Steve told me you have a good aim."

She passed me the pistol, a revolver, and I placed it in my hoodie pocket. Steve hadn't been kidding earlier, she was terrified. We made our way across the dark walkway, taking care not to cause too much of a disturbance. My heart flooded with emotion thinking she had come to get me in her fear. My goodness, she was so afraid that she brought a gun, called the police, and we were heading to her panic room! As upset as I was about Steve, I was devastated at the possibility of losing Maxine. No one had truly cared about me like Maxine.

"Thank you, Maxine," I whispered. "For coming to get me."

"Hush," she said. "Of course I came for you. Marriage or no, you're part of my family, and I'll always think of you as a granddaughter, regardless of what you and Steve decide."

That got tears to well behind my eyes. I gave her a quick hug, and she patted my back. When we got to the main house, Maxine opened the door slowly. The inside of the house felt strange and tense. But maybe that was just me. She nodded to me and smiled reassuringly. She put a finger to her lips.

"I didn't want to scare you, but someone was out on the grounds earlier tonight, creeping around, and it wasn't Steve. Maybe it was Chucky. Steve saw him earlier and said he was angry. But I must tell you, Steve did not answer his phone a little while ago, and I'm afraid something may have happened to our man. We need to move quickly and quietly."

I nodded at her.

"The panic room is in the left rear bedroom, the one Bruno used."

We crept silently down the dark hall, then a very distinct *bonk* made me jump. It had come from downstairs, the game room. Someone was down there. We immediately turned to one another, but in the dark, I couldn't see her expression. She grabbed at my arm.

"Quick," she pulled me. "Let's go, go, go."

Shadows flickered at the end of the long hall, and I knew someone was coming our way, who? Was it Chucky? I suddenly felt like a sack of nerves, and my heart raced. Maxine rushed into Bruno's old room and walked around the bed. All of his things were still there, waiting for him in a little backpack. I couldn't see what

Maxine was doing, but she went to the far wall, stopped, and turned around. I could barely see her small round eyes in the dark. *Where was the door to the panic room?*

"He'll be here any minute," her fearful voice squeaked. "The gun, the gun, get it ready. He's right behind us."

I crowded beside her and pulled out the gun. I held it shakily in my hand and pointed it at the door. Good lord, that heavy metal wanted to slip right out of my grasp. I gripped it tighter. I let my thumb run up the side but there was no safety. Of course not, it was a .38 revolver, and it didn't even have a hammer pullback. I'd need to squeeze the trigger hard. I watched the gun quiver in my hands, and I wanted to pee my pants. *Why wasn't she opening the door to the panic room?*

The bedroom door drifted open, and the shadow of a man filled the doorway. It was Steve. No, it was Bruno. It was one of them. He moved just slightly, and I knew it was Bruno. I felt the panic drain out of me. *He's alive!* Bruno was alive, and safe, and standing right there. I lowered the gun.

"Bruno?"

"Shoot him!" Maxine shouted into my ear. "Shoot him!"

Her shouting made me jittery, and I tightened my grip on the gun.

"It's Bruno!" I stuttered back. "It's just Bruno."

"He's done something to Steve!" Maxine hissed. "What have you done to Steve? What are you planning to do to us?"

His dark form moved one step into the room.

"I've done nothing," he said. "I've only come to gather my things."

"I heard you," Maxine squealed. "We heard you downstairs. You did something terrible. Shoot him now, Amanda, don't let him come any closer!"

But Bruno did come closer. He took another step into the room, and his face emerged from the darkness. He looked terrible in that dark room, hair all out of whack and smudges of something all over his body, dark stains of splattered mess. Were those dark stains blood? Had he done something to Steve? He smelled like mud and sweat and grime. I aimed the gun at his chest.

"I did nothing," his eyes implored me, his voice was soft. "I only wish to gather my things and go home. I waited for the lights to go out."

"Don't let him trick you! He's after the gun!" Her hand clenched onto my arm, steadying me, standing behind me, supporting me, helping me. "Please, Amanda, shoot him before he gets the gun, or we'll all be dead." Her voice whimpered into a wisp.

I didn't know what to do. Her frantic shouts had stirred up my adrenaline, and the darkness pressed down on us. There he stood, with stains of something all over him, standing in a defensive way, tense, and I was scared. *Has he done something to Steve?* The blood pounded in my temples, and I put my finger on the trigger.

"Don't come any closer," I warned.

"Trust your instincts," he whispered.

Was that pounding sound someone running down the hall? Had the police arrived?

I let the gun drift downward, and Bruno sighed ever so slightly.

"What the fuck!" Steve's dark figure filled the bedroom doorway.

In the next second, he tackled Bruno on the bed. The two men flounced around and then one of them fell to the floor. Maxine and I backed up against the wall to get out of the way. Bruno crouched on the floor, and when he went to stand, Steve's foot collided with his gut, and I heard the air rush out of him. He fell against the wall with a loud thud. Steve stepped forward and threw one fist after another in quick succession. He wasn't kidding about those years of boxing lessons. Each punch hit Bruno with sad, hurtful smacks, and with each jab, he cursed.

"Fucking trying to take what's mine?"

Uppercut, uppercut!

"You little fucker!"

Jab, kick.

"Don't ever put your fucking eyes on her again!"

Smack, punch. slap.

He pummeled Bruno, and all Bruno could do was hold up his arms to block the punches.

"Touch anything that belongs to me again, and I will fucking kill you!" Steve shouted, finally tiring and losing his breath.

The moment he slowed down, Bruno's right fist shot out and collided with Steve's nose. One loud crack pierced the air, and Steve cried out and clutched his face. Blood spilled everywhere. Bruno straightened up and threw a couple of more punches. Steve flailed back and fell on the bed. Bruno towered over him with fists clenched at his sides and nostrils flaring.

"Shoot him!" Maxine yelled in my ear.

My head spun around to meet her eye, and Maxine was almost unrecognizable. Her eyes were concentrated beads in their sockets with the most hateful expression I had ever seen. Then, she snatched the gun out of my impotent hand and shoved me aside. Before I could comprehend what was happening, she pointed the gun, aimed, and fired.

The explosion battered my ears, and everything seemed to happen in slow motion. Bruno wobbled back toward the wall. Steve's eyes widened, and the whites formed a complete circle around his iris. Blood splattered on the clean wall, decorating it with scattered droplets. I screamed. Bruno began to collapse. Maxine strutted around the bed with firm sure steps like the majestic woman she was. She held the gun in both hands, steady as a rock.

Maxine towered over Bruno with her feet a shoulder's width apart, pointing the gun right at his head. Bruno stared at her with one hand holding his shoulder, laboring for breath, while his other hand was up in surrender. Blood oozed between his fingers. My heart pulsated at a mile a minute, but I could not move my limbs.

"Maxine!" Steve managed to sit up on the bed. "What are you doing? It's over. Put the gun down."

"I'm going to blow his brains out," she said calmly. "After everything he's done."

"No!" Steve and I said at once. We exchanged glances. His face looked just as scared as I felt.

"No, Maxine, you can't," Steve said. "That's murder. You can't shoot a man when he's down. You'll go to jail."

"I was careful." Maxine released her grip on the gun and held up her hand. "My fingerprints aren't the ones on it."

What?

"Not like that lying, cheating whore's."

What… what did she say? I stared at the soft leather gloves on her frail delicate hands. My scared and weak disposition kept my mind working in slow motion, refusing to accept that she had meant anything nefarious in that statement.

Maxine regripped the pistol and repositioned her feet. She carefully pointed the pistol at Bruno's head.

At that moment, I had an out-of-body experience. It felt like I was watching myself from the sidelines of a football game, unable to control my actions, only able to cheer myself on. Every action was automatic and surprising to me.

I dove at her, causing her to crash to the ground and the gun to skid across the floor into James's room. I didn't care that she had a fragile, ninety-year-old body, and kicked her so hard that she also slid across the smooth wood floors into the hall. I turned to Bruno and helped him to his feet. Out of the corner of my eye, I glimpsed Steve sitting on the bed, holding his nose with murder in his eyes.

Another gunshot rang out, startling us all. Splinters of wood from the door frame rained down on us. Maxine was on the floor in James's room, grimacing in pain, holding the gun in both hands and trying to aim.

"Fuck!" Steve shouted. He rolled over to hide on the other side of the bed. "Maxine, be careful!"

Bruno could barely stand, but I pulled him down the hall, out of Maxine's aim. I struggled to hold him steady and took the brunt of his weight on my small frame. We couldn't move fast, but I kept us moving down the corridor.

"Bitch!"

No, no, no. Maxine stood at the bedroom door holding onto the frame with one hand and the gun with the other. Her face was livid and she stood hunched for the first time in her life. I must have hit her pretty good with that kick. Her round, beady eyes zeroed in on me.

"You bring that boy back here," she demanded. She pointed the gun into Bruno's room. "And you stay in there."

She turned back to me, but we were not waiting for more conversation. Bruno and I booked it around the corner in slow motion. Thankfully, Bruno had begun moving his feet faster.

Chapter 18

The stale smell of iron infiltrated my nostrils, and the sticky wetness of fresh blood covered my hands. The bleeding was not slowing down. It felt slick and thick and was also coming out the back of him. We were leaving bloody handprints everywhere. As we stumbled toward the den, I glanced at his face. His eyes were barely open. His breath came out in moist rasps. Thankfully, it was bloodless drool, and he still had a hand on that wound, slowing the flow.

"Amanda!" Maxine's voice echoed down the halls.

"Amanda," Bruno's weak voice sputtered out in a whisper. "Leave me. Run."

I pulled his frame tighter to my side. My vision was blurred by tears. We made it to the den, and I pulled him toward the French glass patio doors. We could hide out there or go to Chucky for help. A pained hysterical laugh escaped my lips. *We could go to Chucky for help*, my overburdened brain found that hysterically funny, and my stomach clenched trying to suppress my illogical responses.

"Amanda!" Her sharp voice made me jump. "Bring that boy back here."

She sounded stronger, closer, angrier. I only had one hand available to open the door, but it was covered with blood, and the knob was a shiny brushed copper that slipped in my grasp. I realized I hadn't turned the lock, but I couldn't see it because tears were burning my eyes and I couldn't wipe them with the blood on my hands. Then, Bruno's hand touched mine. He unlocked the small deadbolt and twisted the messy knob. The door swung open.

A smashing sound, exploded next to us, followed by clinking as glass hit the ground. Maxine had shot out one of the large windows. I turned to see her standing with the gun in her hand, bent over in pain. Her eyes bore into mine, imploringly.

"Maxine, please."

"This is hurting my hand." She blew out a slow sigh. "I'm an old woman, Amanda. Please hold him steady for me."

"Maxine—"

She painstakingly lifted the gun again.

Bruno tugged me out the door, and I helped him to the steps. He tried to push me forward, but I kept a tight hold of his torso. Behind us, I could hear Maxine grunt as she followed at a snail's pace, stalking us. But we were moving way too slowly, and honestly, even though she only crept, that old woman was gaining on us.

"Amanda," her voice almost sounded normal. "If you insist on helping him, I'll have to do you too. Don't betray a soul sister."

Gravity pulled us down the steps of the patio, all six steps, we fell gradually and painfully to the ground. God, the agony of it all! Bruno gasped in a terrible way.

His face contorted in discomfort, and his limbs shook continuously. His mass was too large for me to pull up without his help, and he wasn't helping me.

"Run," he whispered.

"I'm not running without you." I pulled at his arm. "Bruno, please help me."

Somehow, he managed to stand, and we stumbled toward the dark oak trees. I wasn't sure which way to go and took us toward the river. Maybe we could find a trail and lose her. The crunch of her steps told me she had made it down those porch steps, gaining on us again. *Where's Steve?* Was he still laying on that bed holding his bloody nose? Why wasn't he out here reeling in his grandmother?

Bruno finally collapsed. He rolled up against one of the big oaks. His breath came in panting gasps, and his eyes had narrowed to slits. He clutched his shoulder and pushed me away.

"Go," his voice was very weak, his head was shaking. "You must run."

Another explosion assaulted our ears. Pieces of the oak tree burst around us. She had barely missed his head, though some of the debris hadn't. A large bullet wound scared the tree trunk just left of his ear. I twisted around to see Maxine with the gun.

She must have spent years practicing at the range because she held that thing like an expert; two-handed grip, feet placed to keep her balance, an aiming eye lined up with the muzzle, and a confident expression on her face.

"He came here to steal from me, he threatened me, he soiled our entire family and broke our hearts. I have a right to shoot trespassers."

Bruno coughed and went still against the oak. He was done for the night.

Croquet mallets leaned against the tree. I grabbed one and faced her.

"Put the gun down," I told her.

She let out a snort, relaxing her arm a bit. "Look at you, growing a backbone. Have you made your choice, Amanda? At which table will you sit?"

"You're not getting away with this."

I charged at her, and she raised the gun. With every ounce of strength in my arm, I hurled the mallet at her as if it were a tomahawk, and it cartwheeled through the air toward her head. She wavered, and lost her aim to avoid the projectile causing the gun to shoot high. It hit the tree further up. We were both startled, and like the klutz that I was, I slipped in the grass and fell down about three feet from her. My entire body slammed hard into the ground and knocked me dizzy. Maxine grinned in glee, and my heart sank.

"Dining with the devil is such a poor choice, Amanda." Her beady eyes stared at me. "Especially as your little devil is too weak to help you."

Though her arms shook with the fatigue of firing the pistol, she raised the gun with determination. She pointed the muzzle right between my eyes, and all of the fight drained out of me. I sat frozen with fear. At such close range, there was no way she would miss.

Suddenly, a loud rustle pierced the air, and the flutter of wings swooshed over my head. I stared in wonder as the devil's talons sunk into her old arms, making Maxine cry out in terror. She dropped the revolver and covered her face, but the owl attacked her mercilessly.

The owl hooted while swooping up, then down, pulling at Maxine's hair and ripping it out of her skull. Maxine screamed and moved in a circle. She tried to hit back but only succeeded in getting her hand, her arm, her face clawed. Dark blood coated her forearms.

Maxine stumbled for the patio, but the owl dove down again, and Maxine crashed into the stairs. She slumped down, unmoving, and the owl finally landed on the deck railing. That little devil pivoted its head every which way, then stopped to lock eyes with me, my true soul sister. She blinked twice, flirting with me, then swooped up into the dark night.

Chapter 19

Steve and I were placed in the living area of the big house. Crime scene investigators walked up and down the halls. We could hear them in Bruno's room and also in the other hall, in Maxine's room, running up and down the steps of the back patio, everywhere. Mugs of coffee sat in front of us, but no one was drinking. Steve kept his eyes down, and I kept fidgeting. The entire front of his shirt was covered in blood, and someone said his nose was broken. An hour earlier, an ambulance had taken both Bruno and Maxine to the hospital, but not him. The police did not allow us to go with them. We were first separated into different rooms to give statements, and only recently invited into the den for coffee. I stared at Steve.

I don't belong to you.

His eyes shot to me for a second, and I realized that I must have said that out loud. He blinked his eyes back down to his bruised and swollen hands. They looked painful. Detective Allen finally joined us. He enjoyed a long sip from one of the mugs before speaking.

"Animal control insists the owl only attacked because she was protecting her young in that large oak," he said. "One of the gunshots hit precariously close to the nest, and there's a little chick in there. They're going to leave her be for now. Long-eared owls are an endangered species."

My entire body perked up. "She has a baby?"

The detective nodded. "You were right about Bruno falling into the river," he added. "He apparently went to the dock when he felt strange, to avoid sleeping in the house. He was able to relay that he fell into the water and drifted downstream, ending up on the other side of the water. He purposely laid low, sleeping in the houseboat. He planned to sneak in, get his passport and stuff, and leave."

"Pontoon," Steve said softly.

"Pardon?"

"It's a pontoon, a party boat, not a houseboat," Steve said.

"Yes, the pontoon." The detective fiddled with his computer pad. "It appears that your neighbor Chuck Collins found the man who had been living on that pontoon and dragged him into the station last night. They were quite belligerent, and the desk officer had them detained. But he did send me a message with their statement. After your events here tonight, it won't surprise you to learn that the man accuses Maxine of pushing her grandson over the edge of the levy. He's adamant about it. Claims he confronted her right afterward, but ran away when she threatened him."

Steve narrowed his eyes and slowly shook his head. His hands were folded in front of his mouth.

"I'll confirm the details when I meet them later today." The detective stood. "We'll all meet back here eventually, and I'll let you know what the plan is regarding your grandmother. You might want to have her lawyer present."

The crime scene investigators stayed for hours. They took photos all over the house, the grounds, the dock, and the pontoon. We were not officially on house arrest, but were asked to stay in the area until further notice. I could stay at my bungalow, but the main house was off limits for the time being. Steve said he'd sleep at his apartment.

Later in the day, an Uber ferried me to the hospital. I was anxious to see Bruno, but sorely disappointed when I got there. He allowed the emergency room to bandage him up, but refused to stay at the hospital. No one could tell me where he went. I decided to go back home and start packing my things, wondering where I'd end up next.

Bruno arrived with the detective for our afternoon meeting. His entire left arm was strapped against his torso, and he appear sleepy and sad. His face looked puffy but surprisingly unbruised. His hair was a mess, and he only glanced at me briefly. *Was he upset that I pointed a loaded gun at him in the bedroom?* He followed the detective to the far side of the sitting area, avoiding the rest of us like we had the plague. It hurt to realize that he might be putting me in the same group as Steve and James.

James walked in, back to normal. His stern face was unreadable, but he did exchange a few whispered words with Steve before they found seats. Steve's nose was swollen with a small splint over the ridge. Mr. Daxter was the only one unfazed and chipper, looking like his dapper self. He lounged in his armchair shuffling through several papers one-handed. In the other hand, he held a tall glass of iced tea.

The detective examined his computer pad and cleared his throat.

"I'll just come out and say it," he said. "I spoke to the DA, and it looks like Mrs. Winters will be charged with at least one count of murder as well as attempted murder, among a few other things."

"Hold on," Steve glanced at Bruno and scowled at the detective. "Murder for who? Alex? Are you going to tell me that accusation is based on a bum's ranting? Because that's not going to fly. And the shooting last night, are you trying to call that an attempted murder? Because I think we can all agree Maxine was terrified for her life, and for my life, and for… and because someone broke into the house, that man over there." He pointed at Bruno. "Did you see what he did to my nose? What was Maxine supposed to think? She feared for our lives. I think you're jumping the gun here, Detective."

"Attempted murder of both Bruno and of James," the detective told him.

James stiffened in his chair. Steve stared at the detective.

"Care to elaborate, Detective?"

"Of course." Detective Allen leaned over his computer pad and activated the screen.

The electrical outage had been a ruse, the detective surmised. Someone deliberately turned the power off at the fuse box, likely Maxine. She shut everything down in an attempt to lure Bruno into the house. She knew he was hiding in the pontoon, and patiently waited until Steve fell asleep to enact her plan. Then, she loaded her revolver and fetched me from my cottage. She lured me into the house by saying there was a panic room. Maxine intended for us to encounter Bruno sneaking into his room, where she was certain I'd shoot him out of panic or fear.

"Two birds with one stone," the detective said. "She wanted Bruno out of the picture for good, and she wanted you punished." His eyes met mine.

"What about me?" James said. "Did she put the beta blockers in my insulin?"

The detective nodded. "She did. Our team found a mortar and piston in her back room with traces of her Atenolol all over them. There was a syringe, which she likely used to add the blockers to your insulin container. One of our uniformed officers, Shane Bane, recalled seeing all of you in Old Town for dinner. He was with his girlfriend, a pharmacist, and didn't think anything of it at the time, so wasn't sure what was said. But after the incident with James, Officer Bane asked his girlfriend what Maxine had pulled her aside to talk about. Turns out, Maxine was interested in knowing which of her medications wouldn't mix well with others. She actually asked the pharmacist how many Atenolol tablets were dangerous."

"She put the pills in Aster's tin!" James shouted.

The detective nodded. "Two birds with one Atenolol stone."

And it wasn't just the vagrant's claim incriminating Maxine of pushing Alex over the edge. The crime scene investigators confirmed that one of the prints along the top of the river bank wall matched a pair of the old woman's shoes. They later confirmed that those shoes had traces of mud that matched the riverbank.

That little devil! The devil really was female.

"All of this to keep her money in one big clump," James sneered softly. "All for you, Steve, the golden boy."

After answering more questions, the detective left us alone with Mr. Daxter. None of the three men would look at one another. Bruno stared out the window, James glared at his hands, and Steve closed his eyes. I stood up to leave, but James reached out and grabbed my wrist.

"No! Amanda, stay for this. I'm going to feel better if there's an arbitrary person here."

Mr. Daxter nodded. "Yes, yes, you should stay," he said. "You see, the house was Maxine's sole asset to assign, and she wanted it in your name if you and Steve married."

"Well, we aren't going to marry," I snapped, but I sat down. James gave me a grateful look.

"Then, that settles it," James said. "It's a three-way split."

"Not quite." Mr. Daxter lay printouts on the coffee table. "In my research of the Brazilian paperwork, I found more documents. Official documents. Documents that change everything."

"You mean that handwritten marriage certificate has official documentation?" Steve sneered.

"No, no," Daxter calmed him. "That's still a worthless piece of paper. But there were other documents that are valid." He turned to Bruno with a huge grin on his face. "You brought your birth certificate, but you never told us about your two sisters. Why didn't you bring theirs?"

"He has sisters!" James stared at Bruno. "You mean it's going to be more than a three-way split?"

Bruno rolled his eyes at James, then looked at Daxter.

"I didn't think it was needed," he said softly. "I am here for my mother, at my father's request. My birth certificate is here so that you would know that I am authentic and to help give authenticity to the date of their real wedding, the one you say is worthless. It is my mother who should receive my father's estate, his widow. That is my father's wish."

"It's fine with me," Steve mumbled. "We'll split everything with the sisters too."

"It's not going to be split at all," Mr. Daxter said. "Not unless one of you marry and a baby is in the works. You would need that doctor's note in my box soon, otherwise the entire trust is going entirely to Bruno's mother in Brazil."

"How!" James scooted to the edge of his seat. "That makes no sense!"

"His sister," Daxter looked at his paperwork, "Annamarie is Richard's legitimate daughter, and she's married, she has a baby, and her husband checks off all of Henry Winters's stipulations. It appears they met at Brown University, where she went to school. On the phone, she insisted that any portion of her inheritance be redirected to her mother."

Bruno nodded, the light had come back in his eye. "Yes, yes, that is what she would do. That is what we all want."

"Well, as it stands, that is that." Mr. Daxter stood and nodded to each of us. "Your sister gets it all but has asked for it to be redirected to your mother, so your mother gets the trust. Of course, there is a six-month waiting period, in case anything else changes."

I spent the afternoon packing my things, which didn't amount to much. The bungalow had been fully furnished, so the only items of mine were personal ones that fit into two suitcases. James and Steve were still in the big house, bickering. Bruno had departed with the detective. He was booked on an immediate flight back to Brazil, and he looked eager to leave, obviously desiring to get off American soil as quickly as possible. It hurt that he didn't say goodbye. He only paused to glance at me with a long, sad, closed-lipped mouth. Standing in my living area, my mind kept wandering to him. *Bruno, Bruno, Bruno.* I languished at the window, searching for the devil in the tree as I sipped my tea, my soul sister with a baby. I stirred my tepid liquid with a small spoon.

A dingy spoon.

A tarnished spoon.

An old spoon.

The small spoon in my cup was silver, I realized. It was one of three small spoons that had always been in the cutlery drawer among the other mismatched utensils. Three silver spoons. Could they be the ones he had been looking for?

Epilogue

The Brazilian wine country was startling, and Bruno's younger sisters and mother were beautiful. His baby nephew was terribly cute. They welcomed me into their home with open arms, hugging me tightly like old friends. They chattered brightly and told me Bruno had spoken about me, several times. He described me as a hero, and they expected a larger, physically stronger woman, but I was smaller than all of them, except the baby of course. They giggled at my small stature, but my voice and smile, they declared, he had described perfectly. They all shared Bruno's bright, happy disposition.

When I showed them the newly polished spoons, Bruno's mother cried. They were the family silver she thought had been lost forever. The old family fortune that had traveled from Spain over a hundred years ago. She thanked me for finding them and traveling into another hemisphere to deliver them personally.

She had no clue that it took me five months to gather the passport and money to make the trip. Due to the incarceration of Maxine, I was not paid for my year of ghostwriting. She had been my only gig without a contract, and I learned a valuable lesson with her. Never again will I trust a sweet old grandma-type with my love life, a gun, or a ghostwriting gig… at least not without a contract.

I found the money another way. I completed my thriller in record time, rapidly adding in elements of a tainted medicine container and a dark, midnight shoot-out. My story was immediately picked up by a publisher. I don't want to mention names, but it was one of the big five, and the advance bought me the plane ticket for Brazil.

It took another three weeks to finally get the courage to actually make the trip. I spent the entire flight anxious about dropping in on Bruno's family, but his mother's gratitude made it worth it.

I brought something else to return, I told them, but wanted to give it to Bruno in person. He was at the distilling barn and was due back at any minute. They invited me to wait in the family garden. His sisters were spying on me from the windows of the house, but they were nice enough to give me a semblance of privacy. I didn't mind, because somehow, they projected love to me. I enjoyed a fruity drink and admired the hills of grapes.

The sound of his footsteps crunched on the pebbles that lined the walkways, and I turned to see him, tall, dark and startled. *Bruno, Bruno, Bruno,* exactly the same as in my mind's eye. He wore an open-collar white shirt and slacks. My heart sped up when our eyes met.

"Your shoulder," I blurted nervously, "Has it healed well?"

Bruno nodded.

"I have something of yours," I said.

"Yes, you do. But may I speak first?"

"Of course." I nodded.

My eyes were tearing up, and I didn't know why. Was it because I was so happy to see him? Or was it because I feared coming to Brazil was a terrible mistake?

"Thank you for saving my life." Bruno bowed his head. "I was very angry, confused, and demanded to leave the country right away, but I never thanked you. The hospital had given me many pain killers, and I was not behaving—"

"You had been shot. You nearly died."

He shook his head. "That is no excuse for not thanking you. I should have thanked you right away. I wanted to, later, after I came home and my mind had time to heal. But the lawyer, Mister Daxter, did not know how to reach you."

"I left soon after you did, immediately after the police cleared me. I didn't leave a forwarding address. I also wanted to completely escape."

He nodded.

I took a tentative step toward him and pulled out the giant blue ring with the diamonds, the Paraiba Heart. I had stared at it every day, for months, thinking about Bruno. I held it out to him, and he smiled, admiring the stones. He shook his head at my offer.

"There's something else," he said. "Unless your intent is to return everything, then you should keep it and wear it."

"You mean the spoons? I already gave them to your mother. I wasn't sure if they were the right spoons, but she said they were."

He shook his head. "Not the spoons."

"I'm sorry, Bruno. I didn't find anything else. What else are you missing?"

He took a small step toward me, and the world suddenly felt small, like only Bruno and I existed. Everything else in the universe had faded into the background. I could feel my heart pounding, and I felt faint. He reached out and took my hand, the one that offered the beautiful heirloom ring. I could barely breathe.

"My heart," he said softly. "You also have my heart. If you intend to give it back, I'll accept this ring. But if you intend to keep it…"

His eyes held mine for what felt like an eternity. Then, very slowly, I slipped that ring back on my finger and watched his face brighten as an adorable smile creased his lips. Then finally, shyly, he pulled me into the hug I had hoped to find in Brazil.

The End

Acknowledgments

Thank you to my clan, Bob, Jonna, Annie and Grace for the support and encouragement they deliver on a regular basis. Their insights are always valuable and Jonna's input always strengthens the characters and the stories. I'd also like to thank a few other early readers, Kristina, who weighed in on the plot and gave insightful feedback, and Jamie H. for helping me proofread. Finally, thank-you to Whitney M. for editing my final draft and always fitting me into her busy editing schedule.

About The Author

Joanne Alain Cook is a mother, wife, sister, teacher, artist, officer, and writer. She currently resides in Northern California with her very sweet and handsome husband of 20+years, her beautiful brainy daughters, a goofy Labrador, an angry bearded dragon, three frightened chickens, and a school of clueless fish. Find out what she has in the works at joannealaincook.com.

Don't miss the exciting *Spectral Analysis* Trilogy!

It's more than just ghost story, it's packed with sci-fi, pagan mysticism, feminism, mystery, and romance. Each can be read as stand-alone tales, but are designed to fit together into a larger story arc.

Part 1 - ***Spectral Analysis*** (*seeking lost souls*) A fractured past, entwined with a new inflamed desire, is the perfect combination to aid skeptical Janine into believing the paranormal...but will her enlightenment occur in time to subvert a tragedy?

Part 2- ***Spectral Voices*** (*someone is speaking to spirits*) As fate forces her to face some startling mystic abilities, Janine grapples with how she fits into the greater scheme of things, all while facing unresolved feelings for the man she scorned.

Part 3 - ***Spectral Redemption*** (*the Comba Coven curse*) An ancient curse, reeking of passion, betrayal and murder, force Janine and Kiki to question the men they love, all while ominous events send them spiraling towards a deadly conclusion.

The short extra's, *The Coed Captive* and *True Believers*, are available by request in epub form.